"You're a d...
Detective," ...

Tony's knees nearly buckled. *Concentrate*, he told himself. But all he wanted was to reach out and run his fingers over her cheek and down her neck. She had a little place there that, if he kissed it, would make her melt.

She leaned forward, and for an instant he thought she was going to kiss him. Suddenly she jerked back and turned away, color in her cheeks. "All right, Tony. Let's see if we can turn up any evidence of murder."

She was in her crusader mode, fiery and sincere. And it reached deep within him. He wanted to help, wanted to slay this dragon for her. "You got it, Kel."

Her smile sent a jolt racing through him, making him want things that couldn't be.

Oh, he was in trouble. And it had *nothing* to do with murder....

Dear Reader,

Once again we invite you to enjoy six of the most
exciting romances around, starting with Ruth Langan's
His Father's Son. This is the last of THE LASSITER LAW,
her miniseries about a family with a tradition of law
enforcement, and it's a finale that will leave you looking
forward to this bestselling author's next novel. Meanwhile,
enjoy Cameron Lassiter's headlong tumble into love.

ROMANCING THE CROWN continues with
Virgin Seduction, by award winner Kathleen Creighton.
The missing prince is home at last—and just in time
for the shotgun wedding between Cade Gallagher and
Tamiri princess Leila Kamal. Carla Cassidy continues
THE DELANEY HEIRS with Matthew's story, in
Out of Exile, while Pamela Dalton spins a tale of a couple
who are *Strategically Wed*. Sharon Mignerey returns with
an emotional tale of a hero who is *Friend, Lover, Protector*,
and Leann Harris wraps up the month with a match between
The Detective and the D.A.

You won't want to miss a single one. And, of course, be
sure to come back next month for more of the most exciting
romances around—right here in Silhouette Intimate Moments.

Enjoy!

Leslie Wainger

Leslie J. Wainger
Executive Senior Editor

Please address questions and book requests to:
Silhouette Reader Service
U.S.: 3010 Walden Ave., P.O. Box 1325, Buffalo, NY 14269
Canadian: P.O. Box 609, Fort Erie, Ont. L2A 5X3

The Detective
and the D.A.
LEANN HARRIS

INTIMATE MOMENTS™
Published by Silhouette Books
America's Publisher of Contemporary Romance

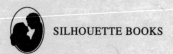 SILHOUETTE BOOKS

ISBN 0-373-27222-7

THE DETECTIVE AND THE D.A.

This edition published by arrangement with Harlequin Books S.A.

® and TM are trademarks of Harlequin Books S.A., used under license. Trademarks indicated with ® are registered in the United States Patent and Trademark Office, the Canadian Trade Marks Office and in other countries.

Visit Silhouette at www.eHarlequin.com

Printed in U.S.A.

Books by Leann Harris

Silhouette Intimate Moments

LEANN HARRIS

When Leann Harris first met her husband in college, she never dreamed she would marry him. After all, he was getting a Ph.D. in the one science she'd managed to avoid—physics! So much for first impressions. They have been happily married for over thirty years. After graduating from the University of Texas at Austin, Leann taught math and science to deaf high school students until the birth of her first child. It wasn't until her youngest child started school that Leann decided to fulfill a lifelong dream and began writing. She presently lives in Plano, Texas, with her husband and two children.

I would like to thank
the following people for their help with this book:

Lt. Dave Davis for his ideas
on how to get a case kicked back.
Warren Spencer for his suggestions
on how police and the D.A.'s office interact.
Robert Hurst of Houston PD for his willingness to
answer all my questions. Any errors are strictly mine.

A dedication:
This is for you, Dad. I miss you.

Chapter 1

"**Y**ou can't go in there unannounced."

Kelly Whalen heard her secretary yell from her desk in the next room.

"You gonna stop me?" The man's tone held true menace.

An assistant D.A. for the city of Houston, Kelly recognized the voice of her ex-husband and wondered why he was here. And apparently unhappy. Very unhappy.

A moment later all six feet two inches of Detective Tony Ashcroft barreled into her office. He wore his let's-frighten-the-socks-off-the suspect expression. "What the hell is going on here, Kelly?" he demanded.

Ash was still an incredibly handsome man with wide shoulders, dark brown hair, and green eyes that sparked with anger.

Teresa Myers, her poor secretary, rushed into the room behind Ash and came to a halt. "Sorry, Kelly. I tried to stop him, bu-but it was like trying to stop a herd

of cattle from charging.'' Teresa knew of what she
spoke, having been raised on a cattle ranch in West
Texas.

''Don't worry about it, Teresa.'' Kelly stood. She
wanted to be at eye level with her ex—as much as she
could—in a position of power instead of looking up at
him like a servant. ''When Ash makes up his mind,
nothing short of calling in the marines could stop him.''

Teresa glared at the detective. ''I don't doubt it,'' she
mumbled as she walked out of the room.

Ash folded his arms over his chest. He didn't look
amused at the exchange between Kelly and Teresa.
''Now that the show's over, you want to explain yourself?''

It had been close to four years since she'd spoken to
Ash. She'd seen him in passing at the courthouse and
around city buildings, but they hadn't spoken since they
had cleaned up the property issues remaining after their
divorce.

''You want to let me in on what *it* is you want explained?'' Kelly shot back, irritated with his attitude.

''Why was I tapped to do the reinvestigation of the
Carlson case since it was originally Ralph Lee's?'' he
snarled.

''What?'' She couldn't believe her ears. ''You've
been assigned the case?'' Kelly felt as if a bomb had
just exploded in front of her, leaving her disorientated
and disconnected to the world.

His eyes narrowed. ''You didn't know?'' He sounded
skeptical. ''Didn't request it?''

''No, I didn't request it.'' Did he think she was nuts?
''And no, I didn't know.''

He crossed his arms over his chest. ''I was called

into my captain's office this morning and told to c-o-o-p-erate with you on this case.''

Kelly hated when Ash got *that* tone in his voice.

''I've been pulled off my active cases, which didn't make my partner happy, and told to report to you. So explain what's going on.''

Taking a deep breath, she said, ''Sit down, Ash, and quit glaring at me. I'm not a suspect that needs to be interrogated.''

''If only it were that easy,'' he grumbled.

She had had enough. ''Just sit down and stop acting like a hard case.''

''I'm the hard case, Kelly?'' His brow arched. ''If I recall, I wasn't the only one.''

She didn't want to open that can of worms. ''This situation is as much a surprise to me as it is to you. I'll call your captain and see what's going on.''

He didn't look as if he wanted to cooperate. He looked more like a man approaching a deadly situation, determined not to let down his guard. He moved to the chair in front of her desk and sat.

Kelly grabbed up the telephone and, with a vengeance, punched in the number of the captain over the detectives. After a couple of rings the captain answered.

''Captain Jenkins, this is Kelly Whalen of the D.A.'s office. Detective Tony Ashcroft is in my office. He says he's been assigned to the Carlson case. What can you tell me about it?''

Captain Jenkins answered in a nonchalant manner. ''Yes, I assigned him the case, Ms. Whalen. Is there a problem?''

Was there a problem? Of course there was a problem. ''Could you explain your reasoning to me?''

''Detective Lee is in Amarillo testifying in a murder

case, then scheduled for a vacation. Since your office needed someone immediately, I assigned the case to Ash.''

"What about Lee's partner?"

"He's retired."

Well, wasn't there another man in the entire department that they could assign this case to? Kelly wanted to yell into the phone, but obviously couldn't say it with Ash glaring at her. "I see. Was there a particular reason you picked Detective Ashcroft?"

"Yes. Ash has just closed several high-profile cases and his caseload is light. And he's very adept at handling the press and the public."

Kelly knew when she was being jerked around.

"Also, Ms. Whalen, you're going to need someone who can stand up to all the different bickering parties in this case. And the man that came to my mind and that of our department lawyer was Ash. Besides, we don't want Carlson or his lawyer to complain that the Houston Police Department tried to railroad their client a second time. Do you have an objection to Detective Ashcroft?" he asked, innocence in his voice.

Jenkins knew exactly what the problem was. She wanted to ask him if he wanted to work with *his* ex-wife in the glare of the TV cameras and radio microphones. Their divorce had been messy. But she wasn't going to let police go one up on her. This was a little game that the police and the D.A.'s office played. Unfortunately, both she and Ash were on the short end of this stick.

"I would've appreciated a heads-up on the situation, Captain." She let her displeasure color her last word.

"Do you want another detective assigned to the case, Ms. Whalen?" he asked again.

"No. Detective Ashcroft will be fine." As she hung up the phone, she gritted her teeth.

She studied her ex over the desk. She could just imagine the sparks that had flown in Jenkins's office earlier in the day. "What did you do to make your captain mad at you?"

Ash clenched his jaw. From his reaction, she'd hit the nail on the head. "Why don't you just fill me in on the case."

Obviously, something had gone down to put him in the doghouse. And although it was a daunting thought to have to work with Ash, she couldn't complain that Houston PD had sent her a bad officer. She may have personal problems with him, but he was a fine cop. And a fine specimen of manhood.

Shaking off the errant thought, she sighed and rubbed the back of her neck. "Last Friday the state supreme court threw out the Carlson case. Reversed and Rendered and the man is out of jail. Apparently, Carlson got a new lawyer and he discovered that one of the jurors knew the victim's parents and was persuasive during the deliberations. Also, the lawyer pressed the issue that the cops had searched his apartment before they had a warrant. The clothing was tossed. I have to refile this case, and I need an investigator to flesh out some new leads.

"My boss is not happy with the court's decision. Andrew Reed is crying foul and raving how his wife's murderer was let out to walk the streets. Catherine's parents, George and Nancy Procter, will probably have everyone on the social register in Houston howling by the day's end and calling every official they know." She mentioned the prominent couple to remind Ash of their problems. "I don't doubt they'll give interviews to every media outlet in the city."

She handed him a copy of her file on the case, then stood and walked around the desk.

Ash opened it. "Ralph Lee was the lead detective?" Ash's solemn tone set her nerves on edge. He looked up and studied her face. From the hard planes of his jaw and cheeks, she had no idea what he was thinking.

"He was, and I'm not happy with the man for doing that search before he got the warrant. He also left several dangling ends. Carlson claimed he was in the Reed house and stole her jewelry, but he didn't murder her. I know I'm going to need another piece of solid evidence that I can give the jury to connect Carlson with the murder. I'm going to need more evidence now that I don't have the clothing I can present to the jury." She didn't mention that there was something in the file that made her uneasy. Maybe once he'd looked at the file, he could identity it.

Ash placed the file on the desk, stood and met her eyes. The air between them became charged. The magnetic pull that was always there between her and Ash sprang to life, surprising and unnerving her. Her heart started to pound and her stomach dropped to her feet.

Why suddenly had the old chemistry that had burned so hotly between them flared to life now? She tried to ignore it, but it was like trying not to see the elephant in the room.

"When Lee finds out about me taking over his case, there's going to be hell to pay."

"Then Lee should take up the problem with your captain. He's the one who screwed up."

Stepping away, Ash mumbled a curse, then ran his hand through his brown hair. The thick waves flowed over his long fingers. She remembered doing the very same thing—running her hands through his hair. She knew how it felt, the richness, the thickness of his hair and what it usually led to.

Stop! her mind screamed.

"Just what I wanted—a fight with Lee and working with my ex-wife on a political hot potato."

His comment jerked her out of her fantasies. What was the matter with her? "Since when did it bother you to go against the establishment?" Kelly snapped. "You always enjoyed poking the powers that be in the eye. And I suspect that was the reason you got assigned to this case. But I need that rebel in you, Ash, to find me something new that I can take to court." She shook her head. "There's going to be a lot of publicity on this case. I won't mention what the mayor had to say about that."

The meeting she'd attended with the mayor, who'd stressed that Andrew Reed and the Procters were powerful in the city's political scene and had supported him, could cause them no end of grief. And he didn't want that headache.

Ash picked up the file folder. There was a question in his eyes and some fleeting emotion that caused her heart to beat faster.

"I'll review this and get back to you."

"I'm going to want to refile this case as quickly as I can."

His brow arched, then he nodded and walked out of the room.

Kelly collapsed against her desk and took a deep breath. She felt as if she'd just finished running a marathon, physically and emotionally wrung out.

She didn't want to work with Ash. It was bad enough

she had to revisit this nightmare. Remembering this case, and what had been going on in her life was painful. Add to that all the political fallout, then Ash being assigned. The captain knew exactly what he'd done by giving this case to Ash.

Ash's husky voice had sent goose bumps rushing over her skin. When they were married, he'd whisper the things he wanted to do to her, and she'd melt into a puddle at his feet.

But that couldn't happen again. They were only working with each other. Period. End of story. Nothing more.

Too bad her body didn't believe that.

Ash marched down the hall of the main police facility, his temper building with each step.

He'd been blown away this morning when his captain announced he'd been assigned to work with Kelly. Then coming face-to-face with her had knocked him for a loop. She was still a gorgeous woman, blond hair, deep blue eyes, and a figure that had stopped more than one attorney at the courthouse.

He pushed open the door of Matthew Hawkins's office and barreled inside. Ash's ex-partner now worked as a lawyer for Houston PD. "What the hell were you thinking, Hawk?"

Hawk looked up from his desk and sat back in his chair. "I've been doing a lot of thinking, Ash. It's kinda the nature of my job. You want to narrow it down?"

"Kelly."

Ash threw himself in the chair in front of the desk. "You know how I feel about—" He gritted his teeth, not wanting to think about his ex-wife and the tide of emotions their meeting had jerked out of him. Dammit. He didn't want to work with her.

Hawk put down his pen and studied Ash. "You're lucky if that's all the fallout from this past week." Hawk shook his head. "Wrecking two cars within six days, then you finish up by punching out the suspect's sister."

Ash glared at his friend. The first wreck had been his fault, running the light as he chased the suspect who got away. The second wreck, the suspect had rammed him. "The woman was trying to stab me in the neck with a nail file as her brother ran away."

"Well, you created a media nightmare, and Jenkins was ready to send you to Pasadena on an exchange program, when Kelly called him. When Jenkins talked the situation over with me, asked me what I thought, what was I to say?" Hawk shrugged. "Your butt was in a sling."

Ash ran his fingers through his hair. "How'd you like to work with your ex?"

"My ex-wife already tried to run that scam on me, remember? And I nailed her on it."

Ash remembered the incident. It was after Hawk had married his current wife, who turned out to be an heiress. "Yeah, Brandy didn't take to kindly to your second marriage."

Hawk shook his head. "She wanted money. But Kelly is nothing like her."

Years ago, when they were still partners, Hawk and Ash had gone through their divorces within months of each other. They drowned their sorrows together and commiserated with each other on the disadvantages of marriage.

Recently Hawk had remarried and now had a child. He was happy with his life for the first time in years.

"It was Ralph Lee's case," Ash grumbled, wanting Hawk to know how truly miserable this situation was. "His screwup."

"I know."

"So just throw me into the biggest, darkest pit you can find."

"I'll admit Ralph can be an SOB to cross—"

Ash's brow arched.

"But you can go toe-to-toe with him, Ash," Hawk finished.

Ash shook his head. "I don't know if I can do this, Hawk. It was weird standing there, looking at Kelly. I haven't had a face-to-face meeting with her since we divided the property." He ran his hands through his hair. He didn't want to admit the feelings that had ripped through him earlier. Feelings that he never thought he'd experience again. And certainly not in response to Kelly.

Ash glared at Hawk. "I don't know whether to punch a hole in the wall or the supreme court jurists for letting Steve Carlson loose."

"My legal advice is that you do neither."

He shook his head. "So not only do I have to work with my ex, I have to dance around Ralph Lee's ego. The man's worse than an old dog with a bone. What a mess."

"You got it."

"You know, since you've discovered love, Hawk, you've become a real pain in the butt."

"Ash, if you need any help, let me know."

"What I need is another A.D.A. and someone else to do this case," Ash grumbled as he left Hawk's office.

"Unfortunately, you're it."

Didn't he know.

"So, that was your famous ex-husband?" Teresa Myers asked as she placed a letter on Kelly's desk, then lingered longer than necessary.

If Teresa only knew what Ash and she'd been through—but she didn't, and Kelly had no intention of sharing. Of course, after this afternoon, Kelly could understand Teresa's awed tone. Meeting Ash under the best of circumstances was intimidating. Meeting him when he was fit to be tied wasn't a pleasant experience.

"That was him."

"Is he always so—uh—dynamic?"

Kelly shook her head. She'd bet that *dynamic* wasn't Teresa's first choice of words to describe Ash. "Pretty much."

"Really?" Her eyes widened.

"Ash is good and doesn't take shortcuts." The words tumbled out of Kelly's mouth before she thought. "If he brings me evidence, I can count on it. And that's what's important right now, not how I feel."

"So, what you're telling me is you are going to be able to work with you ex and have no problems?"

That was the question that had plagued Kelly since Ash had left. "Why shouldn't I?" she answered.

"Because the man's a hunk."

Great, just want Kelly needed to hear. She clenched her jaw and forced a neutral tone. "Ash could strip naked in this office and it wouldn't affect me, except that I would call another cop to cite him for indecent exposure."

Teresa's expression said she didn't believe a word of it. "If you say so." She picked up the newspaper on the desk. The headline proclaimed Carlson's release. "Isn't this going to be a nightmare? My mom asked about double jeopardy."

"If Carlson had been found innocent, that would be the case. This order throws out the original verdict and part of the evidence, so we have to start all over again. I need to refile on this case. Would you bring me the paperwork?"

"Sure."

Once alone, Kelly stood and walked to the window. Downtown workers poured from the buildings, hurrying home. Home to their families and loved ones. Kelly didn't have to worry about anyone waiting on her. She was her own woman. No one to tell her what to do. No one to tell how her day had gone. And she liked it that way.

When she reviewed the case days ago, after the court had ruled, she was distressed with the dangling ends left in the case. Also, although Carlson copped to the burglary, he vigorously denied murdering Catherine Reed. There was fiber evidence to prove he had been in the Reed house, but no blood evidence could be found to connect Carlson with the murder. And it had been a bloody scene.

She shook her head. Working with Ash wasn't going to be a problem, she assured herself, even though their approach to the law was as different as night and day. He thought outside the box. She wanted all the *i*'s dotted and *t*'s crossed. Her miscarriage had intensified those differences, driven a wedge between her and Ash that had finally resulted in their divorce. He hadn't understood—Kelly stopped her thoughts from going further.

Those were issues that weren't involved in this case

and she wouldn't have to revisit them. They could work together on a professional level.

Yeah, and since when did the assistant D.A. start lying to herself? asked a voice in her head.

"Since the Carlson case got kicked into my lap," she whispered.

Ash walked slowly into the building that housed the criminal division of the D.A.'s office. He'd spent the night reviewing the Carlson case. Reed claimed that he and his wife had gone to a society dinner. Then afterward, he had dropped his wife off at their house and gone out for cappuccino at a trendy coffee bar by their house. When he had came back home, he had found Catherine in their bedroom, hacked to death with the Civil War saber that had belonged to Catherine's great-great grandfather. He'd immediately called the police. Afterward, it had been discovered that their safe had been robbed of two diamond necklaces.

All the pieces fit together into a clear picture—except that there wasn't any blood evidence on Carlson or in his apartment. Fiber evidence, yes, but no blood. Of course, Carlson could've disposed of the shirt, but as bloody as the crime scene had been, it would've also gotten onto his pants, too, which had contained fibers.

Carlson's hands had been cut and bruised, but he claimed it was from changing a tire on his car.

What didn't make sense to Ash about this case was that Carlson was a burglar. He'd done time for theft. He didn't have a history of violence, with the one exception of being arrested for hitting his ex-wife. The manner in which Catherine Reed had been killed indicated rage. Carlson's history didn't fit with the crime.

Ash wondered why Kelly hadn't questioned this aspect of the crime the first time around. Then it hit him—the timing of the murder. Five years. Kelly had just miscarried their baby.

No wonder Kelly hadn't questioned the little nagging doubts in the file. He didn't doubt that some of the work he had done right after the miscarriage could have been called into question.

It sounded to Ash as if Steve Carlson had gotten the short end of the stick, and he didn't have a decent lawyer to complain about it the first time around. Kelly wasn't going to be too pleased with his observations.

When he walked into lobby of the criminal division, Kelly stood next to her secretary's desk.

"Good," she sighed, "you're here." She didn't wait on him but walked into her office.

"Is the detective here?" Ash heard someone ask Kelly.

"He is." Kelly stood by her desk.

Seated in the chairs before her desk was an elderly couple. Introductions were quickly made to Catherine Reed's parents, George and Nancy Procter.

"So when are you going to rearrest that killer?" Mrs. Procter asked. The elegantly dressed woman pinned Ash with a hard stare, which belied her soft tone. Her husband also watched Ash with cold regard.

Ash looked at Kelly. "There's a lot of work to do, beginning the case, again. And it's a cold trail, which makes things even harder."

"Do you mean you're not going to arrest that man today?" Mrs. Procter's voice reminded Ash of a queen issuing an order to her servant. Ash had always resisted being pushed or bullied. It was a quirk he'd acquired in the first grade when an older third-grader had tried to bully him. After a week of taking it, Ash had punched the bully and ended the terror. He'd learned a valuable lesson, never to be victimized again.

Ash opened his mouth, but Kelly stepped forward. "We want to make sure nothing else will go wrong and that we can nail Steve Carlson."

"And will you press for the death penalty?" George Procter questioned.

Well, it was certain that the Procters weren't going to be happy unless Carlson fried. Apparently the genteel society folks were out for blood, not that he could blame them. But he had the feeling that the Procters were going to be breathing down his and Kelly's necks.

Kelly leaned back against her desk. "I'll have to talk to my boss about the disposition of the case."

"I want that man to pay for what he did to our little girl," the older man insisted, "and I don't care what it takes to make him pay."

It sounded as if George Procter was ready to take justice into his own hands.

"I'll be sure to pass your feelings on to my boss," Kelly told him.

"There's no need. I'll tell him myself," George informed her. "Come, Nancy, let's go."

After the couple left, Kelly closed the door to her office. She leaned back against the door. "This is going to be a nightmare. I've already had five calls this morning about this case—from my boss, the newspapers, the victim's husband—all demanding to know what I'm going to do." Her gaze met his, and she silently asked if he had the answer.

"Have you looked at the file, Kelly?"

Her eyes narrowed. "I have."

"So you see our problem."

She sighed. "Yeah, I do. That's why I wanted the

case reinvestigated. I need more to tie Carlson to that crime. I want you to go over it again, Ash. Interview the people at the dinner party that night. Something's wrong. I didn't catch it before, but I'm not going to make that mistake a second time.''

''All right. I'll start digging, but you realize, in the intervening five years, a lot of the people who could've helped might not be there. And the evidence from the crime scene, we need to reevaluate it.'' He wanted to paint as dark a picture as he could.

''I know that, Ash. Remember who you're talking to.''

As if he could forget it. He had tried for the past four years to avoid having to deal with Kelly Whalen. He'd been fairly successful in his quest. Until now.

But she had a point. Of all the people in the city, Kelly would know how hard it would be to investigate this murder.

''I know you know how difficult this is going to be. Tell everyone we're going to have to go from square one and it's going to take some time,'' Ash replied.

She rubbed her neck. ''What I need is a miracle. You got one?'' Her eyes begged him to have an answer. That look sizzled down his spine, warning Ash that he was walking into trouble.

A loud rap on the door stopped Ash from answering Kelly. Immediately, the door opened and the D.A. walked into the room. Jake Thorpe, a tall man with a shock of white hair, had made his way up through the ranks. He had joined the D.A.'s office in the early seventies after he got out of the army and had gone to college and law school.

''Ah, good, you're here, Ashcroft. That will make things easier.'' He turned to Kelly. ''I just got a visit from George and Nancy Procter. I must say they were very concerned about the disposition of this case."

"I just bet they were," Ash muttered.

Kelly glared at him.

Jake's brow arched. "What we need to do is make sure you can refile this case. Are we going to be able to do that anytime soon?"

Kelly's chin came up. "Ash was just enumerating the problems we're going to have with the evidence and witnesses."

Jake turned to Ash. "What problems?"

"As I started to explain to Kelly, the case rested on Carlson's confession to the burglary, and fiber evidence on his clothes. With the clothes out, all we have is the jewelry. He could claim the necklaces were given to him. We need to connect him with the murder. Over the passage of time, witnesses have left the area and if we don't have the evidence in storage, then I doubt we can uncover anything new."

Jake studied Ash. "We all understand the problems, Detective. What we need is a new pair of eyes to view the evidence. But we also need you to do so quickly. I can only take so much heat."

Ash understood. Jake was between a rock and a hard place, and he didn't much care for it. He wasn't the only one.

Ash leaned back in his chair and took a deep breath. He reviewed the file Kelly had given him.

"So you've been given my case."

Ash glanced up into Lee's hardened face. The scowl the older man wore was enough to frighten anyone with a lick of sense or guilt. At six foot, two-hundred-and-fifty pounds, Ralph Lee looked as if he could take down any suspect and beat him into a pulp with his ham-sized fists. It didn't matter that the detective was fifty. He was still in top shape, with a steely gaze that had been known to bring more than one suspect to his knees.

"You through testifying in your case in Amarillo?" Ash asked.

"The man took the plea bargain the D.A.'s office offered."

"I thought you were going to go on vacation," Ash replied.

"I heard about the Carlson case and decided to come back. You've been assigned the case?"

"Yeah, Jenkins gave it to me."

Lee's expression hardened. "I'll talk to him." The older man marched into the captain's office. Twenty minutes later, Lee walked out of the office. "I'm going to take my vacation. If you have any questions, you just run it by the captain. It seems he's got all the answers."

Ash glanced at the captain's door. It was open and Ralph made sure he'd been heard.

Oh, things were going to hell in a handbasket.

Kelly settled down in her bed and tucked the blanket under her chin. It was an unusually chilly night in Houston, the damp cold seeping into her bones. Ash had always teased her about being a wimp when it came to cold. When he had been beside her in bed, she never had a problem with cold. It was like sleeping next to a furnace.

"What's the matter with you, Whalen, thinking like that?" she grumbled out loud to the empty room.

It didn't bode well for her if, in twenty-four hours of working with Ash, she was remembering how it felt to be in bed with him.

Not in her wildest dreams had she thought the cops would assign the case to Ash. He really must have made someone mad. She ought to check it out.

Who would have thought a week ago that she'd be facing this political hot potato and have to deal with her ex.

As she stared into the dark, she wondered if she would survive this case? There were wounds that had been inflicted that had never healed, issues that Kelly had never wanted to deal with. That was the trouble with issues—they always managed to crop up at the most inconvenient time. She didn't think Ash was anxious to revisit the old wounds, either; nor did he seem pleased to be working this case. Well, if they came to an understanding to leave the past in the past, then maybe they could work together on this case.

That was a plan. She hoped Ash would go along with it. But then again, when had Ash ever made things easy?

Chapter 2

Ash glanced around Honey's Hideout. The seedy bar, with the uneven floor, chipped tables and grimy walls probably had failed the last four or five health inspections. Of course, the clientele at the bar wasn't interested in food or eating. The liquor this joint served would probably kill any germs.

Sunlight had a hard time penetrating the cloudy windows, but Ash spotted Steve Carlson at the end of the bar, nursing a beer. The man's expression didn't look like one of victory or enjoyment, but rather like a dog that had been kicked one too many times.

Ash had lucked out that Carlson was here at his old hangout. After five years in prison, Steve Carlson's first trip out of his apartment, he had come to this dive—not the grocery store or a job placement office, but this dump. Some of HPD's best business came from here.

Ash slid onto the stool next the man.

"I'm been looking for you, Carlson," Ash began. He pulled out his badge and flashed it at Carlson.

The other man's pinched features hardened. "What do you want?" he demanded. "I've been out of prison less than a week and done nothing wrong." Carlson was a slight man, in his early thirties, five foot ten, thick glasses and thinning hair. He didn't seem strong enough to have butchered Cathy Reed with a saber.

"You want to discuss this in front of an audience—" Ash glanced at the bartender "—or you want to talk in private?" Ash asked, his voice pitched low.

Carlson's eyes went to the bartender, who eyed them, and around the nearly empty bar. "Private."

Ash motioned to a table in the corner of the room. Once they were seated, Carlson demanded, "What do you want?"

"I want to talk to you about Catherine Reed's murder."

"Go away."

Ash shrugged. "Hey, I thought you might want to help clear your name."

Carlson's harsh laugh bounced around the room. "Sure, that's what cops do, try to prove the suspect innocent." He took a swallow of his beer. "If you think I'm going to say anything to you after what you cops did to me, then you're crazier than my last cell mate."

Ash leaned forward. "Think about it, Carlson. There's going to be another trial because of who the victim was. Both Catherine Reed's husband and parents are powers in this city, in this state. They're not going to let this go. They've already been yammering at the D.A. about the situation." With each word, Ash watched the other man's face close down.

"So?"

"So you want a repeat of the first trial?"

Carlson's eyes narrowed. "Why don't you talk to my lawyer?"

Ash leaned back in his chair. "Hey, I got no problem with that. I was just wondering why a pro like you would stoop to murder? I didn't think guys with your talent would hack a women to death."

"Too bad that thought didn't occur to that woman D.A. at my first trial."

"Well, your hands were torn up."

"Changing a flat will do that."

Ash bit back his irritation. "So you saying you didn't do it?"

Carlson glared. "That's what I'm saying."

Ash sat back, considering him. "Makes sense to me."

"Yeah, tell it to the D.A." Carlson swallowed the rest of his beer.

"All right."

Carlson went still, his eyes narrowed. "What's the catch?"

The man responded to the lure Ash had put out. "Well, Catherine Reed is still dead and someone needs to be tried. I thought that maybe you'd be interested in helping me catch the real killer."

Carlson laughed. "Who hit you in the head?"

Ash shrugged. "You're right, Carlson. It is far-fetched for me to believe that you want someone else to pay for that murder. Besides, I don't believe you were ever charged on the burglary. I think the D.A. needs to do that immediately. We're getting grief about you walking around. Of course if you help, those charges can go away. But if you don't want to help…" Ash stood.

Carlson's eyes widened in surprise. "Wait."

Pausing, Ash looked at Carlson.

"What do you want to say to me?" Carlson asked, fingering his glass.

Ash sat and leaned forward. "After reviewing the case, I don't think you killed Catherine Reed."

He nodded. "You're damn straight."

"My problem is, if you didn't do it, I need to find out who did."

"So find him."

"That's why I'm here. I want you to recount that night to me. Maybe you've got the key and don't know it."

Carlson stared at his empty glass. "I should have my lawyer here."

"Fine." Ash pushed away from the table. "We're going to refile on this case soon and if I don't have someone else, you're it."

Carlson knuckled his glass. "What the hell. I broke in the house to rob them. I saw her necklace the week before when I worked a society party, parking cars. I discovered who they were and where they lived. I worked the charity fund-raiser they were at that night. After I parked their car, I cut out and went to their house. She didn't have the necklace in her jewelry box, so I looked for a safe. Found it in the library. I'm good with safes and it was a piece of cake to break into it. I took a couple of necklaces and a ring."

A rush of excitement flooded Ash. "So no one was there when you broke into the house?"

"No. I heard them drive up. The party wasn't supposed to be over until ten. It was nine when the car pulled into the driveway. I heard yelling and cut out. I steal, but don't murder."

Carlson's reasoning sounded firm. Ash knew that thieves rarely changed their modus operandi. When they chose a victim, many professional thieves didn't carry any sort of weapon with them.

Carlson shook his head. "But as I was leaving, I knocked over a plant in the library. I didn't have time to set it upright. Someone else did that lady. It wasn't me."

"What about the murder weapon? Did you see it?"

Carlson's eyes dropped to the table. "I've got a thing for weapons like that. I considered taking it. Took it down from the wall, but I noticed the engraving on the blade. I couldn't fence anything like that, so I left it. But in my hurry, I didn't hang it back on the wall."

There was something about Carlson's story that rang true. "Okay, I believe you."

The look of surprise on Carlson's face made Ash want to laugh.

"You do?"

"Houston PD isn't after you, Carlson. We want who killed Mrs. Reed."

He didn't look convinced.

"I'll want to keep in contact with you in case any other questions come up." Ash handed Carlson his business card. "When you get a job, let me know where I can get in contact with you."

Carlson nodded.

Ash stood and walked out of the bar. Carlson sounded innocent to him. But he had discovered that the Reeds were fighting when they returned home.

It was a new lead.

Kelly packed up the papers she needed to take home with her to review. This day had been a little better than the day the Texas Supreme Court overturned the Carlson conviction but not by much. She had a headache, her feet hurt from standing in court most of the day, and if she had to listen to one more complaint—one more society matron telling her what an injustice had been perpetrated on the state—she might run screaming from the room.

She'd had to get out of her office before anyone else could protest or ask her to do something or tell her what else had gone wrong.

Leaning down to grab her purse, she heard the door to her office open. "Rats," she mumbled.

When Kelly stood up, Ash filled the doorway. His expression didn't bode well for what he had to say. Her plans for escape vanished like smoke.

"I'm warning you," Kelly quickly told him, holding up her right forefinger, "if you're going to give me bad news, don't."

"Have a bad day?" He looked too good for her peace of mind. He had on jeans, a white shirt and an old sport coat that she'd bought him. Her heart jerked in reaction.

"You really don't want to hear about it, Ash." She shrugged her purse over her shoulder, grabbed her briefcase and started out of her office.

He followed her. "Then you're certainly not going to want to hear about what I've come up with in the Carlson case."

She stopped beside her secretary's desk in the outer office, her head bowed. She didn't want to hear the doom he was sure to deliver, but she couldn't avoid it. That had always been Ash's complaint—that she couldn't ignore problems.

"I don't want to know about it right now," she muttered, surprising herself and no doubt her ex. She marched out of the office into the hall.

"When was the last time you ate?" he asked, following her.

His question surprised and annoyed her. She pushed the elevator button and glared at him. "I don't know. Breakfast, maybe. Why?"

The doors to the elevator opened and they moved inside.

"Still not taking care of yourself?"

She glared at him.

"What you need, Ms. A.D.A., is a meal. You still like stuffed crabs?" His expression was smug, as if he knew a secret that no one else did. And he did. She was tempted not to answer, but her stomach growled. "Yes."

"Then let's go get some of Sal's stuffed crabs and fettuccine Alfredo."

If he had asked her to strip naked here in the elevator, she couldn't have been more surprised. He knew the weakness that she had for Sal's crabs. When they'd been married, dirt-poor, her a law student, him a beat cop, they would allow themselves a meal at Sal's once a month. It had been the highlight of the month. Eating at Sal's, a bottle of cheap wine and a walk in the park afterward. It had been heaven, and some of the best times of her life. They were certainly more enjoyable than ninety-nine percent of the official functions she had to attend as a D.A.

It was ridiculous that going to Sal's would hit such an emotional note for her. She was hungry and the stuffed crabs sounded heavenly. If Kelly told him she didn't want the memories Sal's invoked, he might misinterpret it. She was tired, that was all. "All right. You've bribed me."

He grinned, an expression of cocky arrogance. She didn't want to add to that arrogance, but stuffed crabs— it would be a brief reprieve from the lousy day, she told herself. "You going to buy?"

"Will that get you to go?"

"Yup."

"Then I'm buying."

"After you buy me dinner, then you can tell me what ugly facts you've uncovered."

"I will, but only after you've eaten."

Sal's was a little place, the last business in an old turn-of-the-century building with atmosphere that you could scrape off the walls. Ash was sure that, if he pulled the health records on this place, he wouldn't be happy. But on this point, ignorance was bliss.

Sal smiled when he saw them walk into the restaurant. "Ah, Mr. and Mrs. Ashcroft. It's been too long since you've come to my fine establishment. Come, the table you like is empty. I will seat you."

Ash winced inwardly. Hadn't he been here since the divorce? He glanced at Kelly to see her reaction to Sal's mistake. Her face drained of color. She followed the little man without a word of protest.

After they were seated, Sal asked, "Stuffed crabs and fettuccine Alfredo and a sauvignon blanc?"

Ash looked at Kelly. When she nodded, Ash agreed. "I'm surprised you remember what we like to order, Sal, with all the customers you've had over the years."

Sal grinned and leaned down. "I'll tell you a story, Mr. Ashcroft. When you and the missus used to come into my place, I'd tell my wife, look at those two lovers.

There's a passion there that is reserved for the few. Then I would grin at my Catherine and give her a good kiss and a pat. She enjoyed when you came into the restaurant.''

Ash couldn't have been more surprised. Glancing at Kelly, he saw the wounded expression in her eyes. Her jaw clenched. Sal's words had inflicted a serious wound.

''I'll get the wine and turn in your order.'' Sal hurried away.

Ash glanced at Kelly. ''I'm sorry—''

She shook her head. ''It's okay.'' But from her body posture, her shoulders hunched as if to protect herself, it wasn't.

Taking a deep breath, she hid her emotions behind that cool lawyer mask of hers. It was one of the things that had always grated on his nerves.

Finally she shook her head and leaned back in her chair. ''Well, it's just too perfect an ending for today.''

Before Ash could respond, Sal returned with the wine and poured them each a glass.

He took a sip of wine. ''I understand. It's been one of those days for me, too, when you want to kick the hell out of your tires to vent some of the frustration.'' He shook his head, noticing that he had her attention. ''I was tempted, but decided I didn't want broken toes in addition to all the other problems we've got. Besides, dealing with the city when you smash up your car is worse than dealing with the snotty rich kids in the Memorial area.''

Kelly's shoulders relaxed. ''I'm sure the city is grateful you didn't take your frustration out on another municipal vehicle.''

His brow arched.

She shrugged. ''A friend of mine in the department

called today and commented on your trouble." Carrie Nelson, a forensic psychiatrist with the PD, had also given Kelly sympathy about having to work with her ex, even if he was a good detective. "Tell me what you've discovered," Kelly quickly asked.

He was more than ready to move on to another subject. He told her about the conversation he had had with Steve Carlson. "I've got to tell you, Kelly, I believe the man," he told her as the waiter arrived with their dinner.

"Oh, come on, Ash." Doubt and disbelief rang in her words. "I've seen you nail a dozen different guys who were all claiming to be innocent and you brought me the evidence to back up your hunch. What's the problem now?"

He put down his fork. "The problem is the blood evidence. Why wasn't there any found in Carlson's apartment, considering how bloody the crime scene was?"

"That bothered me, too, when I looked over the file."

He ran his fingers through his hair. "Why didn't it bother you the first time, Kelly?"

"It did, but Lee assured me that Carlson could've gotten rid of the shirt. He had the jewelry."

"Yeah, he ripped them off, admitted it, but he claimed he left when he heard the a car coming up the driveway."

From her expression, she wasn't convinced.

"Carlson admitted he was sloppy in his escape, leaving evidence of the burglary."

"So."

"So, if we believe Carlson, then we've missed the murderer completely. He's been walking around for the past five years. Has he killed again?"

Her expression hardened. "Do you have another suspect in mind?"

Grinding his teeth, he pulled a hard rein on his anger. Kelly wasn't the enemy. "I wish I did. I'll interview all the neighbors to see if I can come up with anything new, and comb through the evidence we have. You want to call your people tomorrow and see if they can pull the evidence you've got stored?"

"I'll do it." She cocked her head. "As a matter of fact, we can go over it together."

"Don't trust me, huh?"

"No, that's not it. Maybe your point of view will help me see things in a different light."

What he needed was some time and distance away from this woman. But since that wasn't going to happen, maybe he could make this as fast as possible. "All right. Call me when we can go over the evidence."

"I will."

Of that, he didn't doubt.

Kelly pulled her car into the parking lot of the old warehouse where the evidence from tried court cases was stored. With the darkening shadows and unsavory atmosphere in this part of downtown, Kelly felt her body tense. She wished the D.A.'s office would store their evidence in a police facility. At least cops were there.

When she opened the main door to the warehouse, she saw Ash standing on the far side of the little room, leaning against the counter that separated the waiting area from the smaller office. He laughed at something the male attendant said.

"You're wrong, Ray," Ash answered.

Ash was a handsome man, Kelly admitted, with a

body that would fuel any female fantasy. It certainly had fueled hers once upon a time.

Enough, she mentally scolded. She didn't need to remember *that* about him. What she needed to remember was what a pain in the rear he could be. But that mulish quality of his was what she needed right now, a man not afraid of causing ripples and stepping on toes. And toes were going to be stepped on.

"I wasn't," Ray answered. "And Jeffies got his chops busted when his boss came back."

Ash glanced at her and the grin on his face evaporated. "You're a little late, Kelly."

"It's rush hour, Ash."

His brow arched, silently reminding her that she was the one who'd set the time they were to meet.

She stepped to the counter. "I need the evidence on the Carlson case."

Ray nodded and entered the name into his computer terminal. After several moments, he asked, "You want the door from the bedroom where they found Cathy Reed in addition to all the other evidence?" he asked.

She remembered the door. Blood had splattered on it when Catherine Reed had been murdered. Kelly had kept that door in her office for close to six months, studied it, knew the evidence on it. She didn't want it back again.

"No, since I've got pictures of it in the file. If we need it, I'll send someone over to get it."

"Okay. You got the request form I need to keep?" Ray asked.

Kelly pulled the paper from her shoulder bag. Ray took it and, after carefully looking over it, he nodded and walked through the door into the warehouse.

"Where do you want to go over this evidence? Your office?" Ash asked.

"Yes. I have an opening argument to write, so it would be easier if we did it there."

Ash studied her and she knew he noticed the circles under her eyes. For a moment, his concern showed in his eyes and it caused the oddest sensation in her stomach. The outside door opened, dispelling the moment, and Ralph Lee walked into the building. He carried a box of evidence.

"Ah, if this isn't a coincidence," Ralph murmured. He set down his box on the counter. "The A.D.A. and her detective."

Kelly didn't want to trade insults with Detective Lee. She kept her mouth shut and smiled at him.

"You here to collect the evidence on the Carlson case?" Ralph asked.

"We are," Ash quickly answered.

"You going to right the wrong the state supreme court committed?"

Ralph Lee's thinking had never made it past the seventies, when men ruled every part of the justice system. He was obnoxious but had good instincts on a case.

"We're reviewing what we have and searching for new information," Kelly replied.

Ralph's eyes narrowed.

"And what are you doing here, Detective?" Kelly asked.

"Returning the evidence on the case I went to Amarillo to testify. The assistant D.A. had an emergency and asked if I'd return the evidence."

Kelly felt Ash move behind her. Oddly enough, it was a comfort to have him standing behind her.

The door to the inside part of the warehouse opened

and Ray appeared with a pushcart with two boxes on it. "Here you go, Ms. A.D.A. Evidence in the Carlson case." Ray noticed the other detective. "How are you, Ralph? You got stuff for me?"

"I do, Ray."

Ray held out a clipboard to Kelly. "You have to sign for the evidence."

She quickly signed the sheet. Ash took one box and Kelly the other. Ralph opened the outside door for Kelly. There was an expression in his eyes that made the hair on the back of her neck stand up. As she walked by Ralph, he whispered, "That bastard is guilty."

Kelly stopped. "Well, that may be, Detective, but because we've got to do this again, I want my case airtight. There were some holes when I reviewed it, so Detective Ashcroft and I want to look at the evidence again."

Lee's eyes hardened. "I've got the best damn closure rate in the department."

"This isn't about your closure rate, Detective. This is about convicting a murderer." She walked by him, her jaw tight. "The man is a self-centered, puffed-up, three-eyed monster," she grumbled, walking to her car.

A laugh jerked her out of her fuming. She turned to Ash.

"Ralph has that effect on women. They want to kill him. That's why his partner usually interviews them at crime scenes and leaves Ralph to interview the men."

She shook her head. "Why does HPD keep him?"

"Because, Kelly, he's got good instincts and a good solve rate."

"So he said."

"It's true."

"Then why does this case have holes in it?"

His frown only confirmed her suspicion. "That's a good question."

"If my case had holes, do his other cases have problems?"

She didn't like the look in his eyes.

Chapter 3

Ash cursed a blue streak as he followed Kelly's car through downtown Houston to her office. The little bug she'd put in his ear kept whispering.

And whispering. And what it said left a hole in his gut.

Ralph had a legendary closure rate, one he held over everyone's head. But what if that rate wasn't all it was cracked up to be? What if Ralph had done things in other cases that had helped close them prematurely? Ash's mind shied away from thinking about such things, because if the Carlson case wasn't just an aberration, but part of a pattern in Ralph's closure rate, then they were in deep trouble. If anyone caught wind of this, the courts would be waist deep in prisoners claiming their cases had been railroaded.

He tried to bury the worry as he carried the boxes from Kelly's car to her office. Teresa, Kelly's secretary, smiled coyly at him when he walked into the room.

"Let's go into the conference room, where we can spread out this evidence on the table," Kelly called over her shoulder.

Ash followed her into the room, noticing what a nice butt she had. He tried to ignore his awareness and set his box on the long table.

"Are you going to need me for anything else, Kelly?" Teresa asked from the doorway. She smiled at Ash again.

Kelly looked from Ash to Teresa. "No, you go on home, Teresa. We're fine."

Once they were alone, a warning flashed in Kelly's eyes. Ash shrugged and opened the box in front of him. Inside was Catherine Reed's blouse, covered with blood, different items from the room that had blood on them, a carpet sample from the bedroom and pictures from the crime scene. But the murder weapon, a Civil War saber that had hung on the hall wall outside the upstairs bedroom, wasn't in the box.

Kelly unloaded her box. Evidence from Steve Carlson's apartment, envelopes containing DNA results and samples of blood evidence. Kelly leaned back in her chair, glancing over the items on the conference table. They compared the items on the table with the inventory sheet. Kelly shook her head.

"Where's the saber?" Ash asked.

Kelly looked through her file. "We gave it back to Andrew Reed, since it was a family heirloom and was valued around fifty thousand dollars."

Kelly studied the evidence. "There's nothing here that could be thought of as a smoking gun."

"Let's go over the inventory items."

Kelly read them off the sheet.

Ash surveyed the items. "Nothing different from the file I reviewed yesterday." He shook his head.

"What?"

He forgot that Kelly could read him in ways that other folks couldn't. But that was before she had miscarried and turned inward and they had drifted apart. "The blood evidence still bothers me. I need to investigate it further."

"It bothers me, too." She shook her head. "I should've seen this problem the first time."

He leaned forward, resting his arms on the table. "Kelly, you just went on what Ralph gave you."

"What I did was accept his word and didn't look closely at the case. It was a slam dunk, and I didn't want to see anything else. I was worrying about my conviction rate. Wanted another promotion."

No, what had really been going on at the time was Kelly had just miscarried their first baby. It had been a devastating experience for both of them. This case was the first one she'd handled after she went back to work. He saw that truth in her eyes.

"Let's not panic. There's no magic key here. It looks like I'll just have to start from scratch and reinterview everyone listed here, see if I can develop any new leads."

Kelly picked up a picture of Catherine Reed. "She was a beautiful woman."

Ash looked over her shoulder at the picture of the victim. As much as they tried to divorce their feelings from these crimes and violence, once in a while a case got to you. "She reminds me of my vision of Snow White." He shook his head. "Who'd ever think I'd say that?"

She smiled at him. After a quiet moment, she asked, "Why do I have a bad feeling about this, Ash?"

He shook his head and stood. "That's because there's something wrong here."

A moan escaped her. "Oh, no. Don't tell me that. But I knew…" She took a deep breath. "Okay, Ash. You're the detective. I'll go with your interpretation."

"That's a first." The comment slipped out of his mouth before he could think.

Kelly laughed. The sweet sound made Ash want to kiss that lovely mouth.

Whoa, boy. Don't go there.

Her eyes darkened and the air between them vibrated with their awareness. He stood and took several steps away from her to keep from touching her.

Ash didn't mention that he had doubts about Andrew Reed. He wanted a closer look at the man. Since Catherine's death had been so violent, it spoke of rage. Did Andrew Reed have a problem with anger? What was his relationship with his wife? That hadn't been explored in the previous investigation. And why not?

Terrific, just what he needed, a nasty murder case among the rich and famous.

They quietly put the evidence back into the boxes. "Do you want me to put these boxes in another location?" When his gaze met hers, the electricity in the room exploded between them.

"Uh—" She swallowed. "Just leave them there."

He wanted to reach out and draw her into his arms and kiss her senseless. The thought scared him.

"I'll be in touch." He strode out of the room before he did something stupid.

Ash glanced around the elegant den of Andrew

Reed's mansion. The maid informed Ash that Mr. Reed would be with him momentarily. An original oil painting of the Texas Hill county by J. Williams hung over the fireplace. A photo of the artist, famous in Houston and San Antonio, and Andrew Reed, smiling and shaking hands graced the other wall.

"Do you like my Williams?" Andrew asked as he walked into the room.

Ash looked at the handsome man. Pictures of Andrew Reed with other local celebrities hung on the wall. A president, governor, a couple of senators. But there were no pictures of Catherine Reed. "I'm not much into art. My ex-wife said I had taste in my feet," Ash commented.

Andrew's brow arched. "What can I do for you, Detective?"

"The D.A. wants more evidence for the upcoming retrial. I've been assigned to the case. I want to review with you what happened the night your wife was murdered."

Andrew didn't look pleased. "How long will this take? I'm scheduled to pick up my fiancée and take her to the opening of J. Williams's new art show."

"Probably a half hour."

He glanced at his watch. "Could we do this tomorrow, a.m.?"

Alarm bells went off in Ash's head. "Yes. But if you have five minutes now, I'd like a walk-through of the house so I can visually put it together."

Andrew nodded. "Of course. Follow me." Andrew walked to the library and showed Ash where the wall safe was located.

"After the party, I wanted a cappuccino. Catherine

didn't feel well and wanted to go home. So I left her off at the back door.''

"Did you drive into the garage?''

"No. There's a door in the back that leads out to the deck and pool. She went in that way.''

If what he said was true, then Andrew Reed was, in Ash's book, a selfish bastard who didn't bother with anyone but himself. Ash would never let his wife walk into a dark house by herself. But then again, Ash had seen too many evil things.

"Where did you find her?''

"Upstairs." He nodded for Ash to follow. Once on the second-floor landing, Andrew walked to the first doorway. "She was lying just inside the door on the floor, dead.''

"It was noted that the murder weapon was given back to you after the trial.''

"Yes, since it was an antique treasure.''

"Where is it now?" Ash asked.

"I gave it to the Civil War museum at Rice University.''

Ash observed the bedroom where Catherine's body had been found. Obviously, it had been repainted and new carpeting put down. There were no pictures of the dead woman.

Andrew glanced at his watch. "I have to leave now, Detective.''

As they walked to the front door, Andrew's expression seemed too pleasant. "I'll be sure to block out the time for you tomorrow.''

"Thanks.''

As Ash climbed into his car, he glanced back at Andrew Reed. He hadn't moved from the front door. For a man who needed to get going, he wasn't moving very fast.

Ash smiled and nodded at him. Andrew Reed turned and walked into his house. Glancing around the exclusive neighborhood, Ash decided to start interviewing Reed's neighbors now. He might learn about the Reeds' marriage. There wasn't any mention of their relationship in the file and he wanted to know how things stood on that score.

He got out of the car, closed the door and walked to the next house.

Kelly rushed into the little burger joint tucked on the edge of downtown. She needed to talk to Ash and had called his office, but had been informed he was at dinner. They had told her where.

The evening traffic in this place was strictly folks who worked late at the jail, D.A.'s office and city hall. She immediately spotted Ash in a corner. Their corner booth. When they'd been married, they had often come to this little place for a quick meal together. Since the divorce, she'd only been here once. She walked over to the table. In the past two days, she'd visited too many of their old haunts for comfort.

"Well, Ash, you've lived up to your reputation," she blurted out, not wanting to think about the past.

He rested his arm on the booth behind him. "Exactly what reputation is that? All-around pain in the butt or the tenacious detective?"

"I heard you've been cutting a wide swath through the upper crust of Houston society these last forty-eight hours."

He cocked his head. "Is that what you heard?"

"From more than one source." She leaned forward,

not wanting everyone in the place to hear her answer. "You simply can't bludgeon these folks, Ash." The smell of his hamburger wafted over her and made her stomach growl.

"Sit down, Kelly. I'd planned on going by your office tomorrow, but since you're here—" he shrugged "—we can talk about what I've discovered these past two days."

She didn't like the tone of his voice or the look in his eyes. She slid into the booth opposite him.

"I told you that I probably wasn't the best man for this job. And as I recall, you didn't object to my directness. You wanted it."

She held up her hand. "You're right. And you gave it to me in spades. I've heard from Catherine's parents about you asking their friends and neighbors ugly and tasteless questions about the status of their daughter's marriage."

Ash grinned, obviously pleased with himself. "Tasteless? But true."

She ignored him. "And I've heard from Mr. Reed that you weren't very civil to his fiancée. I think Andrew Reed said you were as cordial as a damn carpetbagger. I assured him that you were a native Texan and had grown up in Galveston."

"What did he say, Kelly?"

"When I told him you were a native, he wondered why you didn't have more genteel Southern manners. Then he decided you must've come from poor white tr—people."

His wicked smile appeared. "What did you tell him?"

"What I wanted to tell him was he was a snob and to stick his opinion in his ear. But what I said was that if he wanted his wife's murder solved and Mr. Carlson back in jail, he needed to cooperate with you and not worry about your manners.''

''What Mr. Reed is upset about is me discovering that he was fooling around with Catherine's best friend. He's probably worried that his spotless reputation with his in-laws might be tarnished.''

She sighed in disgust. ''So that's how the wind was blowing.''

''Indeed. Convenient that Steve Carlson confessed to the burglary. It prevented a lot of dirty laundry from being aired.''

''This just gets better and better,'' she murmured. Her stomach growled again.

He handed her one of his fries. ''Here, start on this while I order you dinner.'' Ash turned to the man behind the counter and yelled, ''Mark, I need another burger.''

''And onion rings and a Coke,'' she added.

A twinkle of mischief sparkled in his eyes. After he yelled out the additional items, he settled back against the booth.

''All right, Ash, what have you got?''

He handed her another fry. ''Andrew Reed is going to remarry next week.''

''Why would that be a problem?''

''He was not a happy camper when I showed up. In that house, there was not a picture of Catherine Reed anywhere to be found.''

''Reed, it's been five years.''

He leaned closer. ''I've thought about it. But wouldn't it make sense that some trace, some memento of his dead wife, of their time together would be around? I mean he played the grieving husband to the hilt at the funeral and trial.''

''Why do you find that so unusual?''

''When my mother died, my dad kept her pictures all over that house until he passed away three years later.''

She frowned. ''But Andrew's case is different. Because of the heinousness of the crime, I wouldn't expect him to have pictures of her around. Just like a divorced couple, I wouldn't expect either partner to have things around to remind them of their ex.''

He didn't respond and Kelly's nerves were on alert. Had he—? She swallowed hard. ''Maybe there's something there you didn't know about. A piece of furniture or picture, something that you wouldn't know about.''

Mark showed up with the burger and onion rings. He winked at them. ''Never thought I'd see you two again, sitting with each other.''

Kelly's eyes widened.

''We're working on a case, Mark,'' Ash explained.

''Oh, is that what those vibes were I felt coming from here? Hey, maybe I should get into police work.''

This was the second time within a week that someone had commented on them being together. She stared down at her burger. Confusion rumbled around her head. What was going on?

''The point I'm trying to make, Kelly, is that Andrew's neighbors said that within weeks of the murder, he had someone come in and redo the entire house. Nothing of Catherine remains.''

She took a bite of her burger and thought. ''Still, Ash, it's not that unusual a response to a death. A violent death.''

''Well, you wanted my gut reaction in this case. There it is. Also, this fiancée is the second one he's had since his wife died. The society woman he was seeing while Catherine was alive expected to be the next Mrs. Reed. She was very shocked when Andrew dumped her.''

''Ash, I wish I could charge Andrew Reed with being a louse, but we generally don't prosecute things like that. If we did, I'd have to charge over half the male population of the city with it.''

''When I interviewed the neighbors, I got a picture of a couple that fought frequently. Loud. Yelling and slamming of doors going in and out of their house. I also discovered Mr. Reed liked to spend money. And his business wasn't doing well.''

Kelly lost her appetite. She pushed away her plate. ''Why didn't Ralph Lee come up with this evidence?''

''Because he conveniently had a suspect that had confessed.''

''You're going to need to go back and talk to Steve Carlson, again.''

''You want to go with me?''

''Yes, that way no one can accuse you of being biased if I'm there to watch and record the interview.''

''Let's do it now.''

There wasn't a reason on earth they couldn't do it tonight. Except it meant spending more time with Ash, at night, surrounded by darkness and breeding an air of intimacy. ''All right, I'll follow you to his apartment.''

''Don't trust my driving, Kelly?''

''When the interview is finished, I can go home. It's got nothing to do with your driving.''

And it had nothing to do with spending time in a car with him. Nothing at all.

When they arrived at the apartment building where

Steve Carlson lived, they parked in the dimly lit lot. Several people stared at them as they walked up the outside stairs to the second-floor apartment. Ash knocked. There was no response.

"He's there," a little girl told them as she moved away from the door of her second-floor apartment.

Kelly smiled at the child. "How do you know?"

"I saw him let another man inside. Then they started to yell. Later, the man came out, but the other man didn't." She shrugged, then started to jump rope.

Ash looked at Kelly. "You think I've got reasonable doubt that something's wrong?"

"I do. See if the door's open."

Ash drew his gun, then tried the knob. The door opened easily. They walked into the small apartment. There was no sign of anyone in the living room. The kitchen and dining area were empty. And neat. In the bedroom they found Steve Carlson, lying on the floor, staring at the ceiling, a bullet hole in his right temple. A gun lay inches from his hand.

Ash looked at Kelly. "Why do I get the feeling this case has taken another ugly turn?"

"That's because I doubt Steve Carlson killed himself."

"Which means that someone wanted to shut him up."

"Or, Ash, maybe someone wanted our investigation stopped. With Carlson's death, that would be the logical assumption."

"But you're not going to quit, are you, Kelly?"

She looked back at the body, then at him. "Give me a reason to continue, Ash. Give me the evidence I need."

"All right, I will."

Chapter 4

Kelly stepped back against the kitchen counter and watched the police evidence team work the scene. Ash stood inside the bedroom door, carefully observing the activity. He glanced at her, and they both knew the trouble they were facing.

A commotion outside the front door drew Kelly's attention, and she saw the news reporter.

"You can't go in there," Kelly heard the officer tell the woman.

"I want to interview someone in charge about this murder. It's big news." The young woman looked into the apartment. She caught a glimpse of Kelly. Unfortunately, Kelly knew her.

"Ms. Whalen, can you tell me what's going on here? Isn't this the man who was just released from prison, Steve Carlson? And why are you here?"

Kelly didn't want to talk to the eager-beaver reporter, but had discovered the hard way the more you tried to dodge the press, the more they pursued you. She walked to the front door. "Hello, Amber. I accompanied one of the detectives here." Kelly didn't mention she and Ash were the ones who had found the body.

"Is Steve Carlson dead?" Amber shoved the microphone in Kelly's face and the cameraman behind her started taping.

It was better for the situation if Kelly gave the reporter a minimum of information. Squinting because of the camera light, Kelly answered, "Yes, Steve Carlson was found dead in his apartment."

"Was he murdered?"

"At this point, I don't feel free to supply any more details. The police haven't finished working the scene. Further details will be released later."

Amber frowned. "Can you comment on the method of death?"

"You'll get all the information you need from the police information officer," Ash interjected, his tone hard and professional. He stood behind Kelly, a solid, welcome presence.

Amber ignored his silent warning. "Can you tell me anything more?"

"No."

Any sensible person would have understood the danger in pressing her case. Apparently Amber didn't fall into that category.

"But this is important for the public to know. What happened?"

Ash glared at young reporter and said nothing. He pushed his way through the reporter and her cameraman. Kelly followed.

"Damn press," Ash grumbled as he walked down

the stairs. He stopped by his car and glanced around the parking lot.

When the captain had mentioned that Ash was good at dealing with the press, Kelly had wondered what the man had been drinking. She felt fortunate that Ash had simply walked away from the confrontation instead of blistering the young woman for her stupidity. He had done so in the past with other reporters.

He ran his fingers through his hair. "Sometimes I wonder where they dig up these little wonders."

"I'll give you brownie points for waiting until you were out of earshot to make your comment."

His head came up and his eyes locked with hers. A hint of humor twinkled in his eyes. "Yeah, well even this old dog can learn a new trick."

He didn't look like an old dog. Instead, he looked like a strong presence that she could depend upon. She shied away from the thought. "You going to interview Carlson's neighbors tonight?"

"Yes. I'm waiting for my partner to help."

"You have a new partner?" Of course he had. The last partner she knew about was now a lawyer with HPD, advising the department on legal matters. She purposely had not kept up with Ash's career.

Suddenly two sedans pulled into the parking lot. From one car emerged a well-muscled man in his early forties with a steely-eyed gaze. A woman got out of the second car. Tall, shapely and very pretty, the woman's blond hair was pulled back into a ponytail. Was this Ash's partner? A stab of jealously knifed through Kelly.

The captain over Homicide nodded at them. "Ms. Whalen."

"Captain Jenkins."

"Ash, what do we have here?" Captain Jenkins asked. He wore a want-to-chew-nails expression.

"Kelly and I wanted to talk to Carlson. When he didn't answer the door, a neighbor—" he glanced at Kelly to see if she would point out their witness was a little girl, but she remained quiet "—assured us that he was there, that she'd seen Carlson and another man enter the apartment, then heard them argue. The other man left. I felt the circumstances warranted entrance. We found Carlson dead on the floor of his bedroom."

His expression hard, Captain Jenkins turned to Kelly. "Detective Ashcroft had your opinion on the exigent circumstances?" The good captain wanted the department's rear covered.

"He did and the circumstances were urgent."

Captain Jenkins nodded. "Show me where you found the body."

Ash, Captain Jenkins and the woman turned and started back toward the building. Ash paused. "Kelly, are you coming?"

She wanted to go, to make sure everything was seen to, but she wouldn't appreciate the cops trying to tell her how to try a case. "What's happening is your job. I'm going home. I'll let the D.A. know about Carlson."

A gleam of admiration flickered in his eyes, then he nodded and turned. As she watched him go, Kelly knew things were going to get ugly if they continued the investigation into Catherine Reed's murder. Everyone would expect the inquiry to stop with Carlson's death, but neither she nor Ash wanted to let it go. It wasn't finished. The case had just taken an unexpected turn.

Ash didn't understand why he was here, parked in front of Kelly's house—*their* home pre-divorce.

His skin prickled as the air of familiarity washed over him and a thousand memories assaulted him. What the hell was he doing here?

He came to fill Kelly in on what he'd discovered from the neighbors, he told himself. Share with her what the lab techs thought about Carlson's death, and nothing else.

Liar, a voice in his head whispered. *You could've done all that with a call tomorrow morning.*

He didn't have an argument against that truth. Instead, he walked to the front door. The color had changed. It was no longer a mud-ugly brown. Now a soft peach graced the wood.

He knocked and heard steps in the entranceway, then the door opened. Kelly stood there in a robe of some soft material that clung faithfully to every curve. He cursed under his breath.

You're batting a thousand, Ashcroft.

"Ash, what are you doing here?" She held a cup of coffee.

"I thought I'd fill you in on what we discovered." It sounded lame to his ears.

Her level of interest intensified. "Did you turn up something significant?"

"No." He felt as if he was six years old and had stumbled in front of the entire school at the Christmas pageant. "It seems no one saw anything, but that didn't sit right with me or my partner, Julie."

"Julie?"

"You goin' to make me stand outside for this entire conversation? I doubt the neighbors want to hear about the Carlson murder." He glanced around at the other homes.

"You're wrong, Ash," she grumbled. "Everyone

wants to hear about it, from my boss to Mrs. Schattle.''
The elderly woman was the neighborhood's busybody.

Apparently things had already gotten sticky. ''So you
want Mrs. Schattle involved?'' he asked.

Her cheeks reddened. She stepped back and motioned
him inside.

Ash glanced around as he walked into the living
room. She'd replaced most of the hand-me-downs
they'd been given. New sofa and chairs.

''You mentioned Julie. I assume that was the woman
who arrived at the crime scene with Captain Jenkins.''

Julie had laid into him for his lack of manners in not
introducing his partner to his ex. He'd argued there
hadn't been time, but his conscience hadn't bought that
excuse. When Julie left the crime scene, he told her he
would introduce her to Kelly at their next meeting. Julie
had laughed and told him she was over the slight. She
assured him that she wouldn't introduce him to her former boyfriend and to forget it.

''Yes, it was,'' he answered.

''What did she think about the crime scene? She
think it was a suicide or murder?''

''She agrees with our conclusion.''

''It's nice to know you and I aren't that far off the
mark.''

He leaned against the wall inside the door. ''Both of
us had the feeling that our little witness wasn't the only
one who overheard this exchange between Carlson and
the other man, but no one is talking. I think we might
have better luck in a couple of days when the entire
building isn't crawling with cops. Julie is good at putting witnesses at ease and getting them to talk.''

Kelly held the cup close to her chest. His gaze locked
onto her chest. ''You want a cup of coffee?''

He thanked heaven she misinterpreted his gaze. "Sounds good."

He followed her into the kitchen. Kelly poured him a cup, then opened the refrigerator door for an exotic-favored coffee creamer. "Want some?"

He frowned and stepped closer, grabbing the cup. "No."

She shrugged and poured a little more into her cup.

He didn't remember her liking her coffee smothered in cream. It emphasized that time had moved on and they were both different people. "Why even drink coffee if you put that much funny milk into it?"

She glared at him. "Because I'm an A.D.A. and not a cop. And I need the caffeine to stay awake. I've got work." She took a sip and sighed. "What did the lab guys say?"

"They were going to run tests on Carlson's hand and temple to see if there was any gunpowder residue. But they agreed with us that it didn't look like a self-inflicted wound. The body position looked staged."

He took a sip of the dark roast. "You mentioned you heard from your boss. What did he say?"

She shook her head. "When I got home, I found a message on my machine from Jake. It appears he saw the news flash earlier in the evening. He wanted an explanation for what we were doing at Carlson's apartment."

From her expression, Ash guessed that Jake Thorpe might have done more than politely ask for an explanation. "What'd did he say?"

She hesitated.

"You might as well tell me it all. We're in this together, and I'm sure I'll get mine tomorrow."

"You mean your boss didn't nail you tonight?"

"He wasn't happy that it was me who found the body." Damn fool had been Jenkins's exact comment, but Kelly didn't need to know that.

From her expression, she knew he had gotten grief but didn't press the issue. "I think Jake talked to your boss, because I got the same reaction. He wanted a report from the scene. He didn't want any more trouble with this case than we've already had. Apparently, the news flash on the local stations reached a lot of people. Carlson's lawyer called, upset. And the Procters also called."

"I'm sure they weren't upset." He leaned back against the counter.

"He didn't say."

"It seems like all the little parties in our case have checked in."

"Except—" Her eyes met his.

"The grieving husband."

It spoke volumes about this mess. It made Ash want to gnash his teeth. Damn, Carlson had gotten the short end of the stick, again.

Kelly wrapped both hands around her mug. Her fingers flexed, making Ash wonder if she was that worried about the case, or maybe it was something else.

Yeah, like sex. He shook his head. It just proved that men never grew out of their youthful fantasies.

"There are any number of reasons why Andrew Reed wouldn't have seen that broadcast," she said. "I'm sure he'll know within a few hours. But I won't be surprised if he never contacts the D.A.'s office again."

"You nailed it." He studied her, wanting to know if she still felt the same way she had at the crime scene. "You still want me to look into this, Kelly?" He wanted to hear her confirm her earlier desire to unravel the inconsistencies of this case.

She put down her coffee cup but didn't look at him. "I remember times when you pursued a case where the evidence indicated one thing, but you went with your gut feeling. It was a headache for the D.A.'s office, but you were generally right. This just doesn't feel right, does it, Ash?" She raised her head and her gaze locked with his.

His entire body went on alert. This was not the time to be thinking with his hormones. But deep inside, he felt a certain satisfaction that she had acknowledged the validity of his hunches. "No, it doesn't feel right."

She nodded. "Okay. Let's get the autopsy reports and see where it takes us."

"You got it." He downed the last of his coffee and set the cup in the sink. A memory of another time, when he and Kelly were married, washed over him. He'd come home late after a brutal investigation. They'd shared coffee, then had fallen into bed together. She'd made him forget for a few hours the ugliness of the crime.

As he walked to the front door, he caught a glimpse of her bedroom off the main hall. From what he could see, that room hadn't changed. Odd.

What was even worse was his reaction to that knowledge.

The door beyond their bedroom was closed. That was the nursery. He wondered what he would find if he opened that door. He didn't want to know.

He reached for the front door. "I'll give you a call when the reports are back in." He didn't turn around to look at her. He didn't want to see the light shining through that robe again. He'd already had too many shocks tonight. He didn't need another one.

Captain Jenkins appeared at the door of his office. "Ashcroft."

Ash glanced up from the morning report. His partner hadn't come in yet. He moved to the captain's office. The corner room had windows and natural light, but files and papers cluttered his desk.

"Yeah, Captain, what can I do for you?"

"Since the D.A. doesn't need you anymore, you can go back to your caseload. Julie's been assigned a couple more cases since you've been working with the D.A."

"I plan to follow up on the Carlson case," Ash informed him. He might as well alert his captain to what was going down.

Jenkins went still. "Why?"

"Because, Captain, Kelly and I both suspect Carlson was murdered to shut him up."

"And why do you think that?"

"Because our investigation was making folks uncomfortable. I know Andrew Reed hated my questions about his relationship with his wife. And he definitely didn't like questions about the night of the murder. Acted like I was out of line to be questioning him again."

"I want to read the file."

Ash nodded. "Carlson would've been indicted again because of the social pressure, but now that he's dead, people will assume the Houston PD won't need to investigate any further into Catherine Reed's murder. I'm sure Andrew Reed is breathing a sigh of relief, along with the Procters. When I talked with those fine, upstanding citizens, they were ready to take out Carlson themselves—or have it done."

Captain Jenkins sighed. He was the one who caught the fallout of the politics of the situation. "You're a pain in the butt, Ash."

"I know, but I'm right."

Jenkins pointed his finger at Ash. "You just be sure I've got paper to shove in the elected guys' faces when they come and complain to me."

"I'll do it."

"The D.A. on board with this?"

"A.D.A. Whalen is on board if I can show her evidence."

"I also want the D.A. apprised of this. I don't want any of us to get our necks chopped off."

"You got it." Ash walked back to his desk. He'd just opened the newspaper when Ralph Lee walked into the room. He paused by Ash's desk.

"How's the Carlson investigation going, Ashcroft? Turn up any new leads?"

Ash looked into the older man's face. In his eyes was a certain satisfaction. "You haven't seen a newspaper or the TV?"

"No. I just got back in from my vacation in the Big Bend area. I stayed away from all media for good reason."

Ash picked up a copy of the *Houston Chronicle* and pointed to the story below the fold on the front page.

Ralph raised a brow and glanced at the story. "I guess the little rat couldn't take the heat anymore."

Ash didn't comment. The statement didn't deserve a comment.

Ralph turned and walked to his desk, leaving a bad taste in Ash's mouth.

Ash slipped into the back of the courtroom and sat

in the last row. Kelly stood before the witness stand, interviewing the middle-aged man.

"So, Mr. Jones, you say you saw the defendant arguing with his wife."

Ash watched as Kelly walked toward the witness. Her dark navy suit couldn't disguise her curves. The simple lines only emphasized her figure. She still had the best-looking backside he'd ever seen.

The first time he had laid eyes on Kelly, he'd watched her walk down the stairs in a lecture room where they had both attended a criminal justice class. She'd brushed by him as she slipped into the row of seats. That good-looking backside had been shoved in his face. If she'd known what he'd been thinking, she never would've agreed to go with him to get coffee afterward.

"What did you hear the defendant say to his wife?" Kelly asked the man.

Her legs, encased in dark hose, were a man's fantasy. They certainly had been his.

Enough, Ashcroft, he commanded himself. *You keep that up and you won't make it through this case with all your marbles.*

"He said that he'd rather kill her than let her have all his money."

She nodded. "Thank you." Turning, she glanced at the gallery and saw him. She hesitated, then walked to the prosecution table. "I don't have any further questions for this witness."

The defense attorney questioned the witness but couldn't shake the man's story. Kelly had probably prepared the man for this line of questioning. She was good in the courtroom. And passionate. She believed in the law, in doing what was right. In that, they thought alike. Their passions ran the same.

And in bed—

He stopped the thought. He kept running over this track again and again. What was wrong with him? It shouldn't have mattered after five years. He didn't need any more grief than he already had. Why didn't he just shoot himself in the foot? It would probably be less painful in the long run.

"We'll adjourn until two," the judge said, bringing his gavel down.

Kelly stood and glanced over her shoulder. She nodded to him, then collected her papers. He waited for her by the door.

"What are you doing here, Ash?" she asked as she met him at the double doors.

"I've got the autopsy report on Carlson. I thought we might go over it."

She raised her brow. "All right." She walked to the elevators.

When the doors opened, Matthew Hawkins stood on the inside. He nodded to both Ash and Kelly.

"What are you doing here?" Hawk asked Ash.

"Chatting with the A.D.A., per your recommendation," Ash replied, glaring at his ex-partner.

Kelly remained quiet.

"I heard about Steve Carlson. Makes things messy. Was it a murder or suicide?" Hawk asked.

Ash met Kelly's gaze, then turned to Hawk. "That's not clear. Kelly and I are going to talk about the case."

Hawk's gaze pinned Ash. "That's interesting."

The elevator stopped on the ground level and the doors opened. Kelly plunged into the waiting crowd. Ash nodded to Hawk.

"See you later." Then Ash followed her into the sea of bodies.

She walked out of the courts building and crossed the street to the offices of the D.A. He followed her into her office. Teresa smiled at him.

"Hello, Detective." The woman put out signals. He wasn't in the mood. "It's nice to see you."

Ash walked into Kelly's office. She placed her briefcase on the desk.

"So tell me about the Carlson case."

It had taken the coroner a week to do the autopsy on him. Ash held the file up. "Ted was his effective self and put a rush on it."

She leaned back against her desk and crossed her arms. "So what does it say?"

He handed her the file. "There was gun residue on his hand and temple."

Kelly opened it and studied the file. "So he ruled it a suicide?"

"No."

She looked up from the report.

"There was a bruise on the back of Carlson's head. Coroner can't say if the blow to the head was before or after the gunshot. Also, the powder residue on his hand indicates something else was covering the victim's hand."

Her brow arched. "Like another hand?"

"It's possible."

She looked down again at the report. He stepped closer to point to the paragraph he wanted her to read. He could smell her shampoo, soap, the natural aroma of woman. And felt his reaction in his gut. He cursed.

"So the ruling is inconclusive?" She glanced up. Her lips were inches from his.

"It is."

Her eyes sparked with the knowledge they'd been right. "So that means we might have a murder."

"It means that the Carlson case isn't closed even if the suspect is dead. We still need to investigate Catherine Reed's murder. It's likely that the two murders are connected."

Kelly Whalen still had the power to take his breath away. When her eyes lit with excitement and she smiled that knowing grin, he was powerless to resist her. Ash wanted to reach out and run his fingers over her cheek and down her neck. She had a little place on her shoulder, right at the base of her neck, that if he kissed it she would melt. Her small breaths and moans when he licked that tender skin thundered through his memory.

"You're a dangerous man, Detective."

His knees nearly buckled. Concentrate, he told himself. "Sometimes you've gotta use the system to your advantage for the good guys."

She leaned forward and, for an instant, Ash thought she would kiss him. Suddenly she jerked back and turned away, but there was color in her cheeks. "All right, Ash. Let's see if you can turn up any evidence of a murder."

"Which one?" He wanted her to face him and tell him which murder they were going to do.

She turned. "Both. I think I owe it to Steve Carlson to unravel this mess."

She was in her crusader mode, fiery and sincere. And it reached deep within him. He wanted to help, slay this dragon for her. Besides, he didn't like attempted coverups.

"You got it, Kel."

Her smile sent a jolt racing through him, making him want things that couldn't be.

Oh, he was in trouble here. And it had nothing to do with Carlson.

Chapter 5

Kelly glanced at her watch as she walked into the police headquarters building. Ten o'clock. She was on time for the case law session that she was required to teach this morning. Instructing any policeman who wanted to update their knowledge of current law. It was Kelly's turn to lecture to the department, and it couldn't have come at a worse time.

It had been a long morning already. Everyone in Houston had an opinion about the Carlson case. She'd heard from certain individuals more than once. But she hadn't heard a peep from the grieving husband.

Every media outlet in the city wanted to talk to her. She'd told them that the ruling from the coroner was inconclusive and the police would continue to look into Carlson's death. She didn't doubt once that information hit the public, she'd have another round of displeased prominent citizens yelling at her.

As she walked toward the elevators, Ash emerged

from a side hall. Beside him was the little girl who had told them about Steve Carlson being in his apartment. A woman, probably the girl's mother, held the child's hand.

Ash nodded at Kelly. She stepped to his side and smiled down at the little girl. "Hello, young lady."

"Kelly, you remember our young witness, Sarah Mendoza." He squatted and looked directly into the girl's wide eyes. "Sarah, this is Assistant District Attorney Kelly Whalen."

Sarah shyly looked at Kelly and nodded. "I remember her."

"And this is Sarah's mother, Rosa," Ash continued.

Kelly offered her hand to the young mother. Rosa Mendoza didn't look happy with the situation, but she shook Kelly's hand.

"Sarah just spent the past hour with the police artist," Ash explained. "And she did an excellent job."

The news encouraged Kelly. "So we have a picture of the suspect?"

"We do. Sarah was very helpful."

The little girl beamed. Ash lightly squeezed Sarah's elbow.

The action touched Kelly's heart. Ash had always been good with children. "Thank you, Sarah, for your help."

Rosa Mendoza pulled Sarah's hand. "It is time we go home."

As they walked toward the front door, Sarah glanced over her shoulder and waved at them. Kelly felt her heart jerk. Her little girl would have been four. A knot settled in her throat. Turning to Ash, she noticed a hint of longing in his eyes. Was he thinking about their daughter?

He quickly buried the emotion. "What are you doing here?" he asked.

"I'm giving the monthly case law session today. Are you going to attend?"

A speculative light entered his eyes. "What's your topic?"

"Current rulings on traffic stops and search and seizure."

"I kinda got the benefit of your knowledge of the law when we were at Carlson's apartment," he teased.

"Yeah, and I've heard no end of complaints about that," she grumbled, and started toward the elevators.

"What's happened, Kelly?"

Before she could answer, the elevator doors opened. She walked into the interior. "You coming?"

"I can't. Stop by Homicide before you leave, and I'll show you the picture Sarah came up with."

As the doors closed, she saw Ash glance at the main entrance where Sarah had disappeared. She had the oddest feeling that little girl had touched his heart. She certainly had Kelly's.

Ash walked to his desk. The bank of windows gave him a panoramic view of the city of Houston. Fifteen floors up allowed them to see the ship channel. Julie McKinney glanced up from her desk across from his.

"You got the picture of the suspect?"

He handed her the composite drawing that the police artist had done. Julie took the paper from his fingers.

"I can understand Rosa Mendoza's reluctance. He looks like a nightmare." She returned the picture.

The suspect had long hair, penetrating, deep-set eyes, and a scar on his left cheek. "I've given the composite to the watch commander. Patrol will be on alert for this guy.''

"What about having patrol keeping an eye on the apartment complex in case the suspect goes back to cover his tracks.''

"I've already made that request.''

She leaned back in her chair. "Did the mother give you a hard time after I left?'' Julie had talked the mother into coming to headquarters to allow her daughter to work with the police artist. Julie had been called out on another case, and Ash had to take over. Rosa Mendoza hadn't liked it, acted as if he would eat her child.

"Let's just say that Mrs. Mendoza doesn't care for male policemen. I probably couldn't have talked her out of a burning building. I was lucky the police artist was a woman.''

Julie grinned. "My heart bleeds for you, Ash. Poor man couldn't charm a woman.''

He blew off her sarcasm and glanced at his watch. Forty minutes had passed since he and Kelly talked in the lobby.

"Has A.D.A. Whalen been by?'' he asked.

Julie rested her arms on her desk and studied him. "Now why would she stroll by Homicide? Is there something you're not telling me?''

"You're treading on thin ice, partner,'' Ash warned.

She arched her brow.

"Kelly is giving this month's case law session. I see you didn't take advantage of our continuing education,'' he admonished.

Julie rummaged through the papers in her in-out box. Finally she pulled out the month's lecture topic.

"You're right. She was scheduled." She put down the sheet and went back to her work.

So much for his partner's continuing education. When Julie McKinney had first been assigned to be his partner, he hadn't wanted any partner. She was his third partner. His second partner, the one after Hawk, had died of colon cancer. Ash hadn't been in the mood to team up with another detective, but he hadn't been given a choice.

Julie hadn't taken any static from him. She pulled her weight and had a finely honed intuitive radar. More than once, she had picked up on something that he'd missed and given them the key to solving a case. Now he couldn't imagine working without her.

Ash sat at his desk and pulled out the Carlson autopsy. He'd bet a month's salary that Carlson had been murdered.

"Well, if it isn't A.D.A. Whalen. What are you doing here at police headquarters?" The sarcastic voice belonged to Ralph Lee.

Ash's head jerked up. Kelly stood in the hall facing Ralph.

"I gave the case law session, Detective." She spoke in that lawyer tone that usually made Ash grind his teeth. Oddly enough, he found it funny that Kelly used *that* tone with Ralph. "I didn't see you there."

Ralph's eyes narrowed. "I'm sorry I missed it. I'll be sure to make it to the next session."

She nodded and walked into the large room. Ralph Lee followed her. The militant look in Kelly's eyes told Ash that she was fighting her temper. He knew not to cross her at this moment. She stopped by Julie's desk and held out her hand.

"Kelly Whalen."

Julie took her hand and introduced herself.

Kelly turned to Ash. "We need to talk to your captain."

Alarm shot through him. In her present mood, he didn't know what to expect. "Why?"

"Because I want you back. Exclusively to finish the investigation of Catherine Reed's murder. And Carlson's, too."

Chills raced over his skin and his heart hammered.

Everyone in the room stilled and every eye settled on them.

Ash stood. "Let's go."

The door to the captain's office was closed. Ash knocked.

"Enter."

He opened the door and motioned Kelly inside before him.

Captain Jenkins stood. "Ms. Whalen."

"We need to talk, Captain." She took the seat he indicated.

Jenkins flashed a look at Ash, silently asking what was going on. "What's the problem?"

"I need Ash back, full-time. I want him on the Reed case and the Carlson case, exclusively."

"Why?" Jenkins asked.

"Because, Captain, our questions have raised hell. The D.A.'s catching it, and I know the police are getting it, too, having just run into one of the devils. The more Ash looked into things before Carlson was killed, the louder the protest." She sat forward. "Something stinks, worse than the chemical leak we had last spring. I'm not going to be intimidated." Her jaw flexed.

Damn, she was something. When his mouth lifted in a grin, Captain Jenkins glared at him.

Jenkins turned to Kelly. "Is your boss in on this?"

"I'll convince him. He's got more on the line than any of us civil servants. Don't worry, I'll make my case. Besides, Jake doesn't like being jerked around any more than the rest of us."

Captain Jenkins didn't look convinced.

"I'll take the heat, Captain," Kelly offered, "and shoulder the blame."

Captain Jenkins looked from Kelly to Ash. "You in on this?"

He would have no problem working exclusively on these two cases. It would be a luxury...*because he'd see Kelly.* He tried to ignore that thought, but couldn't. "Yeah, I want in."

"I'm not sure your partner's going to be crazy about this."

"Let's ask her," Ash suggested. He stood and called to Julie. She appeared at the door.

"Yes, Captain."

Jenkins explained about reassigning Ash back to these two cases exclusively. "You got a problem with that?"

"No. I've been working some cases with Hayes, so Ash isn't up to speed on them. I'll just finish those without him."

Captain Jenkins nodded. "A.D.A. Whalen, have the D.A. call me. I don't want to be blindsided with this situation. I want to know we all have the same goal."

"You've got it."

As they left the captain's office, Kelly murmured, "It looks like you're mine now, Ash."

Oh, that brought a different image to mind than he was sure she meant.

Ralph Lee stood outside the door, his expression cold.

* * *

Kelly pushed open the lobby door of the police building and sailed outside.

"Let's eat," she called over her shoulder, suddenly ravenous. "Why don't we eat at Jim's? I've found myself craving one of his burgers, again."

Kelly didn't even question why, after three years of abstinence, she had a craving for the big greasy burgers at the diner by the jail. She didn't wait for Ash's response but plowed into the bodies on their way back to work.

Within two strides, Ash was at her side. "You're in a big hurry. Are you *that* hungry?"

She glanced at him. "I am."

She knew what that revealed about her. Always after a big test or, later in their marriage, after a high-profile case, Kelly had an enormous appetite. And food hadn't always satisfied that craving.

She felt Ash's gaze on her. She didn't doubt he wondered what was driving her.

People filled the coffee shop. Kelly looked around for a table and smiled when a couple stood and walked out. Ash motioned Kelly before him. She collapsed into the chair.

"Well, look who's here again," the waiter commented. "What's going on? I don't see y'all for years, then suddenly you're a hot item. Have anything to announce?"

Kelly wanted to strangle the guy.

"C'mon, Mark, give us a break," Ash grumbled. "I told you the other night we're working on a case."

Mark nodded. He took their orders, then cleaned off

the table. Once they had their coffees, Ash leaned forward. His gaze snagged hers.

"What's going on, Kelly? What set you off like a Roman candle back there in the squad room?"

She stared into her coffee.

"And don't try to fob me off with some polite excuse. I've got my butt on the line just like you do."

The problem working with Ash was that he knew her, knew her true feelings.

"C'mon, Kel. Be honest with me."

When she glanced up, his gaze captured hers and electricity raced through her body. That look could drag secrets out of her, and she didn't want to own up to the anger driving her. But he deserved to know.

She forced her eyes away from his. "I ran into the Procters' lawyer outside the lecture room."

"Who would that be?"

"The estimable Walter Moen."

"The son?"

"Nope. Daddy. He was very polite, but told me in no uncertain terms he wasn't happy that we were still asking questions about the Procters' darling daughter and her marriage. What could I possibly gain from the exercise except to feed my prurient interests?"

"Prurient?" Ash asked.

"It still irks me that miserable, shriveled-up old man—"

Ash laughed. His humor punched a whole in her anger. A responding laugh bubbled in her.

"I wanted to tell that man I wasn't interested in Andrew and Catherine's sex life because I didn't have—"

"Yes?"

Before she could say anything more, their burgers

arrived. She busied herself with pouring ketchup on her fries.

"What did you tell Walter Moen?"

The knowing look in Ash's eyes made her crazy. She couldn't just tell him that she'd dated a couple of times since they divorced but no man had pierced the wall she'd built around her heart. And she certainly hadn't slept with any of those men. Ash was the last man she'd made love to. But not in a million years would she admit that.

Neither was she going to back down from the challenge in his eyes. "I told Mr. Moen that he knew as well as I that ninety-nine times out of a hundred, when there's a murder like this, there's a problem in the marriage. And in the majority of those cases, it relates directly to sex. Or money."

Ash took a bite of his burger. "And what was the exalted lawyer's response?"

Kelly grabbed a fry, dipped it in the ketchup and popped it into her mouth. Oh, the comforting taste. When she opened her eyes, Ash's gaze stabbed into her. "Uh...he assured me this wasn't the case."

A snort of laughter burst from Ash's lips. "You need a scorecard to keep up with those rich folks. And I don't doubt the hypocrite has his own liaisons." He took another bite of his hamburger. "So, you've decided to pursue this thing, come hell or high water or the society set."

She sighed. "I'm right and you know it."

"I do."

His agreement surprised and delighted her. She popped the last of her hamburger into her mouth. "Okay, let's go talk to my boss and let him know the fallout of the afternoon."

And she prayed she still had a job.

"Apparently, hell has just frozen over," Ash murmured as they walked into Kelly's office.

Kelly whirled to face him. "What is that supposed to mean?"

He shut her office door and leaned close. "An elected official did something bold." The D.A. had just informed Kelly and Ash they could proceed with the investigation of both Catherine Reed's and Steve Carlson's murders. "We can proceed with the investigation."

"Carefully," she whispered.

He smiled at that one condition. "I know how to tiptoe around fragile egos. I can be very good and you know it." His looked down into her face. She still had the most beautiful mouth. Full lips that tasted like wine and honey. The first time they'd kissed, it had nearly knocked him on his butt.

Her eyes widened in shock and she swallowed.

His fingers ran down her cheek, then smoothed a stray hair off her cheek. He wondered how long her hair had grown. Each time they'd been together, she had her hair pulled back into some sort of a twist. He itched to take it down and run his fingers through it. The little piece of information she had let slip earlier at lunch, that she wasn't involved, gave him a heady sense of satisfaction. It also gave him other insane ideas.

A knock on the door broke them apart. The door opened and the secretary stepped into the room.

"Kelly, here's the report you asked for."

Ash knew an excuse when he heard one. He wondered if Teresa had picked up on the vibes between Kelly and him. The pheromones nearly knock him on his keister.

Kelly accepted the folder and retreated behind her desk. "Teresa, Detective Ashcroft is going to need a desk. What's available in the office?"

"That's not necessary, Kelly. I can work in the conference room and keep any papers here in your office."

Teresa's expression fell. "There's an empty office on the other side of my desk. If the detective would like to work there, no one would object."

"Why don't you go and check out that office? It might work better for you instead of the conference room. That room is in use constantly and you wouldn't have any peace or privacy."

Ash knew exactly what his ex-wife was doing. She wanted him out of her office. Their little tête-à-tête scared her. Well, he couldn't blame her. "Sure, why don't you show it to me, Teresa."

The young woman looked entirely too pleased with the idea. "Follow me."

As he walked out of the room, he stabbed Kelly with a look that said he knew what was going on. Ash felt like a zoo animal as he walked through the office. The lawyers and secretaries stared at him. He didn't believe his reputation deserved the reaction he got, but who knew what Kelly had told them about him.

"This office just became available last week," Teresa informed him, stepping into the small office. It had a simple desk, file cabinet, a couple of chairs. But it had carpet, a plant, which he had no doubt Teresa would water, and a view.

"What do you think, Detective?"

He thought he'd been saved. He wouldn't be in Kelly's way and they had just proved that they needed space.

"I think, Teresa, you've come up with a workable solution to our problem."

She beamed and stepped close. "Good." She lightly brushed his arm. "And if you need anything else, you let me know." The expression on her face told him what direction her mind had wandered.

"I'll remember that, Teresa."

"Good."

"Will this work, Ash?" Kelly's voice rang out.

Teresa and Ash turned to find Kelly by the office door. Her disapproval glowed in her eyes.

"I'll get back to work," Teresa mumbled, and rushed out of the room.

Kelly didn't say anything, but turned and walked back to her office. He followed and slammed the door shut behind him. He reached for her.

She jerked out of his hold. "What you saw, Kel—"

"It's none of my business." The look on her face didn't match her words. "But I don't want you involved with any of my staff."

"Then maybe you should talk to your secretary. She's the one who has been sending out signals that she wanted something more than a friendly hello."

"And you have to respond?"

The situation was going to hell. "I wasn't responding. I was being polite. I don't want to hurt her feelings."

"Oh, I just bet you don't."

"I can handle the situation myself, Kelly."

"Why don't we review both the cases and see where we are and what our next step is?"

What he wanted to do was finish the little business he and Kelly had going before they were interrupted. It was stupid and he knew she wouldn't go for that, but that didn't stop the want.

"Sure, let's see what we can come up with."

She looked relieved.

Too bad she didn't want to finish what they'd started. He had the oddest desire to do just that.

Chapter 6

Wondering who'd hit him in the head with a board to scramble his brains, Ash pushed open the door to police headquarters. That had to be the only explanation for his thoughts over the past few days. What the hell was he thinking—wanting to kiss Kelly? If he was honest with himself, he wanted to do more than just kiss her and that shocked him speechless.

Ignoring the ugly truth, he walked to the elevators. He needed to see if his partner could help him interview witnesses in the River Oaks section of the city. Julie was better at schmoozing with the vaulted of society than he was.

"Hey, Ash, how's it going?" David Lyons, a patrolman, greeted him. Ash had investigated a murder in which David was the officer who'd found the body in the park.

"Can't complain," Ash replied.

"I heard you were working with your ex-wife." His brow arched. "How's it going?"

Gossip ran rampant in the department. Sometimes, it was worse than a small town. But, then again, the cops were a small city within the larger population of Houston.

"As well as could be expected."

David shook his head. "Better you than me, friend." He nodded and walked toward the roll call room.

Ash didn't doubt every individual within the department knew of the situation, which didn't improve his mood. Now, not only everyone in the D.A.'s office had him under surveillance, but his buddies here were watching with a jaundiced eye. Added to that were the privileged of this city, who felt they didn't have to talk to a common detective. Great, just what he wanted, three different and various groups waiting for a misstep.

When he arrived at Homicide, his mood could only be described as dark.

Julie glanced up from her desk. "What foul wind blew you in? Did the D.A. shoot you down?"

Ash threw down the file he carried. "No, I came to see if I might talk you into helping me interview witnesses connected with Catherine Reed's murder."

"So if you're still in business there, why look like you want to start a fight?"

He glared at his partner. "You try working with your ex."

"Kelly giving you problems?" Confusion rang in Julie's voice.

"You want to help me or grill me?" he replied.

Understanding registered in her eyes. Wisely she didn't comment, for which he was thankful. Not only could Julie handle suspects with ease, she could weather his moods.

"Sure I'll help." She stood and grabbed her suit jacket. "Let's go."

They said nothing on their walk to the parking lot.

"What did you and Kelly came up with this afternoon?" Julie asked as soon as they were outside.

He welcomed the question. "We wanted to check out the state of the Reeds' marriage. In the file it didn't list any friends they'd interviewed, so we decided to question all the guests at the party Andrew and Catherine attended the night of her death. That's where I thought you might be able to get more information from these folks than me."

Julie laughed and glanced over the hood of his car. "It's not that you can't deal with those people, Ash. It's that you choose not to. You're like my cocker spaniel—you don't give a snort."

He resisted smiling, but he admitted she was right. This time, he was even more inclined to not put up with prissy rich folks. "I'm not the only one. Kelly had just run into the Procters' attorney minutes before she showed up in Homicide." He grinned, the thought lightening his mood. "She was fit to be tied." He started the engine and pulled into traffic.

"Sounds like you and Kelly have a lot in common."

Too much, Ash thought.

The drive to the River Oaks section took less than fifteen minutes. This section of the city was old money—which for Houston meant from the thirties. They quickly found the large mansion and asked to see Mr. and Mrs. Ackers. They were shown into the library. The wood-paneled room screamed of wealth and breeding. Riding trophies sat on the mantel and a large photo of Mrs. Ackers and her prized Arabian hung over the fireplace.

A young, handsome woman in her mid-thirties walked into the room. Ash guessed she must be wife number two or three, because he knew John Ackers.

"What can I do for you, detectives?" she calmly asked, looking at Ash.

"We need to ask a few questions about the night of Catherine Reed's murder," Ash answered, realizing that Mrs. Ackers might prefer to talk to a man.

"Why are you still investigating her death? Didn't her killer die?" She glanced at Julie, then back at Ash.

"He did, but we need to tie up some loose ends," Ash explained.

Mrs. Ackers didn't look convinced, but took a seat on the couch next to Ash.

"We know, Mrs. Ackers, that Steve Carlson worked as an attendant here parking cars the night of the murder. Other things might have been stolen from your other guests. We wanted to put an end to this mess," he explained, hoping to disarm her suspicions.

"I haven't heard of anyone else having a burglary that night." She pressed her mouth into a tight line. After a moment, she sighed. "There were close to two hundred guests at the event, Detective."

"Could you tell me what you remember of the party, Mrs. Ackers?" Julie asked, jumping into the conversation.

Mrs. Ackers leaned back. "Catherine and Andrew arrived late. I only saw them briefly. After about an hour, I heard a commotion. I rushed in here and heard Cathy tell Andrew to 'go to hell,' then she stomped out of the party. He followed."

"Do you know what they were fighting about?" Ash questioned.

She looked as if she had just tasted something unpleasant. "Andrew's mistress was at the party."

This was news to Ash.

"I didn't know about the liaison at the time, but after I heard Catherine and Andrew fighting I sought Cathy out." Mrs Ackers looked up, guilt coloring her eyes. "She told me about the situation."

"How did the fight start?" Ash asked.

"Apparently Catherine found the two of them in a compromising position in here."

"What's this woman's name?" Ash asked.

"What's going on in here?" demanded John Ackers as he strode into the room. He was close to sixty and overweight. His bald head and small eyes proved to Ash that money could buy almost anything, as demonstrated by his wife sitting next to him. She did have a nice rock on her finger.

Leaping to her feet, Mrs. Ackers rushed to her husband's side. "John, these are detectives with the Houston police. They wanted to know about the party we had the night of Catherine's death."

"When I talked to George Procter, yesterday, he assured me that all this nonsense was finished." As John glared at them, Ash suddenly had a feeling that the man had other fish to fry besides the investigation into Catherine Reed's murder.

Ash opened his mouth ready to inform Mr. Big Bucks that he had a job to do, but Julie beat him to the punch. "No, sir. There are some questions we still need answered. Your cooperation would be greatly appreciated."

"I don't want my friends disturbed," John replied.

"We don't have a choice in the matter," Ash answered.

"But I do. If you want to talk to me, contact my lawyer." He clamped his hand around his wife's arm and pulled her from the room.

Ash and Julie looked at each other.

"Well, it wasn't your technique this time," Julie commented.

"I know. Apparently, there's more than one secret out there."

The housekeeper appeared in the doorway. "I'll show you out."

They followed the older woman to the front door. As she opened the door, she stepped closer to Julie and whispered.

Julie stopped and studied the woman, then nodded. They were in the car before she spoke.

"Andrew Reed's mistress was Joanna Kris."

Ash paused. "The housekeeper told you that?"

"She did."

"I knew you'd get the info I couldn't. Now all we have to do is find Joanna's house."

It took them only twenty minutes to discover where Joanna lived. Her home was two blocks from the Ackers. When they knocked on the front door, Joanna answered it.

Julie explained why they were here. "Sure, c'mon in. I'll talk to you about that pig." Joanna stepped back and motioned them inside.

Ash arched his brow, signaling to Julie that this could be a gold mine. They walked into the house, then followed an unsteady woman to a lush den and living room. She flopped onto the couch, then patted the cushion next to her. "Why don't you sit down, Detective Ashcroft?"

He didn't glance at Julie, but felt her amusement. She silently dared him to take Joanna up on her offer. He did.

Leaning back, Joanna smiled and asked, "What do you want to know about that miserable SOB?"

"Were you and Andrew Reed lovers?" Ash began.

She nodded. "We were."

Ash glanced at Julie, then back at Joanna. "And now it's over?"

"Yup, it is," she groused.

"We heard from other sources Catherine Reed discovered you and her husband in a compromising position at the party given by the Ackers on the night of her death. You want to explain to us in your own words what happened?"

She picked up her drink and took a swallow. Ash could smell the tequila. "I told Andrew it was foolish to try anything in that library, but he brushed off my concerns." She shook her head. "I don't think Andrew expected her to make that big a scene. She did. Looked like her world had ended."

"Why wouldn't he expect his wife to complain if she found you and her husband *in delicto flagrante?*" Julie asked.

Joanna's chin came up. "She knew he was straying. Besides, an indiscretion isn't unusual in this community. If you want to stay married to money, you swallow your pride and take what they dish out."

"Is that what you did?" Ash asked.

"My husband was glad to have a young woman on his arm. It was the price he paid."

"Let's get back to Catherine Reed," Julie interjected.

"What did she do when she caught you and her husband?"

"She probably wouldn't have made a scene. But she was with several other people when they walked into the library. She stared at Andrew and said he'd regret his actions, then turned and walked out of the room." Joanna finished her drink, then threw her glass onto the coffee table.

Julie jotted several notes on her pad.

"What was your reaction when you heard of Mrs. Reed's death?" Ash asked.

Joanna rested her head on the sofa cushion. "I thought that I'd be the next Mrs. Reed."

"What happened?" he asked.

She rolled her head toward him. "The bastard dumped me six months ago. Found a younger, more nubile woman. He's such a jerk, he can't keep his pants zipped."

So the mistress had been cheated on. It wasn't an unusual or unique story. They'd investigated more than one instance of multiple betrayals and the murders that had resulted.

"Were you surprised by Catherine's death?" Ash pressed.

She studied her hands, pressed her lips together. "Yes. It was a shame that man killed Catherine."

Ash leaned forward. "Which man are you talking about?"

Suddenly Joanna appeared stone-cold sober. "Steve Carlson."

"Did you see Steve Carlson at the party?"

"No." Joanna stood. "I have an appointment."

Ash glanced at his partner. He wanted to press Joanna about her story, but Julie shook her head.

"Thank you, Mrs. Kris, for helping us," Julie said.

Joanna quickly shook Julie's proffered hand and walked to the entrance hall. As they passed by the grand piano, Ash noticed a picture of Andrew Reed, the mayor of Houston, the quarterback from the Rice Owls, with Joanna settled among the men.

Ash picked up the framed photo. "When was this picture taken?"

Joanna walked back into the room. "Five years ago." She took the picture out of his hand and held it to her chest.

"That's a lovely dress you have on," Julie commented.

"Thank you."

Ash waited for her to add to her statement, but she didn't say anything more. After being so forthcoming earlier in the interview, Joanna's lips had suddenly clamped shut. What had happened?

She rushed to the front door and opened it. There was nothing they could do but leave.

"Thank you for you help. You've been very cooperative." Ash smiled, trying to ease the woman's nervousness.

No response. He took his business card out of his shirt pocket and handed it to Joanna. "If you remember anything else about that night, call me."

She nodded. He stepped outside and the door slammed behind him.

"So what was it that she let slip?" Julie softly asked Ash as they walked to their car.

"She lost it when you asked if she was surprised by Catherine's death."

They slid into the car. Ash thought about the exchange while he pulled out into traffic. "She did close up after that."

"She sobered up and wanted us gone," Julie added.

He nodded.

"You're lucky I took good notes so we can ferret out what spooked her."

"Don't you find it odd that she would keep a picture of a man she thought was a pig on the piano in her living room?"

Julie touched her forehead. "The love-hate relationship some people have is beyond me. I think she still cares for Andrew, but wanted to get back at him for hurting her. She's worried that she might've gone too far."

"It's amazing how often we have to deal with the fallout of jealousy. Tell me who is the next party-goer we're going to interview?"

"Mr. and Mrs Samuel Waters."

Ash shook his head. "We're not going to miss any bigwigs, are we?"

Weariness pulled at Kelly. The day's court questioning had not gone well. The defendant's lawyer seemed to have witnesses to counteract all of hers. The victim's grieving mother had been matched by the defendant's sobbing mother, sister and grandmother. She pushed open the door to the D.A.'s main office.

Jake Thorpe stood outside the door to his private office. When he saw Kelly, he motioned her into his inner sanctum.

Her heart jerked, wondering what he wanted.

"Close the door," Jake instructed.

It was going to be bad. Jake rarely dressed down his staff in public.

She carefully shut the door.

"What in the Sam Hill is going on, Kelly?" he demanded.

"What are you talking about?" She didn't know what had happened, but she'd bet her next month's salary it had to do with Ash.

"I'm talking about your ex making Houston society scream to high heaven."

All sorts of scenarios that made her blood run cold darted through her mind.

"I have Samuel Waters calling me and asking why the police want to know who's sleeping with who in polite society. He didn't appreciate being asked about dirt on his fellow country club members."

Kelly's stomach sank.

"And then there was George Procter calling again about his daughter being maligned." He paced around his desk. "That call was followed by the grieving husband's." He stopped and locked gazes with Kelly. "You know to whom I'm referring."

"Andrew Reed."

"He was livid, assuring me that I wouldn't make another election if he had anything to say about it."

Kelly collapsed in the chair in front of his desk. "I'm sure Ash didn't—"

"Mrs. Delacorte called—"

She raised her hand. "Jake, you gave us the go-ahead to investigate these cases. I thought you understood that we were going to air some dirty linen."

"What you're doing is digging up dirt on every rich oilman in this city, alienating every political patron who's ever supported me. Kelly, this kind of stink can't happen again."

"So you want me to drop these cases?" She wanted

to hear Jake put into words exactly what he wanted done.

He gritted his teeth. "No, dammit. But that doesn't mean this kind of behavior can continue. Come up with another way to interview these people. And do it immediately."

"Let me talk to Ash and we'll devise another method to get at the truth."

"Go."

She stood and walked to the door.

"How'd it go in court today?"

She had gone through another high-profile case. It was the second day of the trial. The star high-school quarterback had produced reasons as to why he wasn't responsible for the death of his girlfriend, who'd been beaten to death. "I may be oh-for-two today, Jake."

He didn't comment, simply nodded.

As Kelly walked past her secretary, she ordered, "Would you get me Detective Ashcroft on the phone?"

Teresa didn't say anything but picked up the receiver. Apparently everyone knew things had gone in the toilet.

After several minutes, Teresa buzzed Kelly. "I can't reach him, but left a message to call you."

"Thanks." Kelly sank into her chair and closed her eyes. What else could happen today?

Ash strolled into her office close to seven. "You lawyers don't do overtime, do you? Now the poor police, we work twenty-four-seven." He smiled, amused at his own humor.

Kelly's head jerked up. Ash looked too good to be as much trouble as he was turning out to be. He had on a sport coat, white dress shirt and gray slacks. At least he'd dressed up when he interviewed all the society folks of the city.

"What's wrong, Kelly?" He strolled to her desk and hitched a hip on the corner.

All sorts of conflicting emotions raced through her. She wanted to punch him for all the grief he'd stirred up—she couldn't count on both hands all the complaints. She'd known he'd be trouble, but was it worth it?

"Kelly?"

"Where would you like me to begin, Ash? You want me to start with the seventeen-year-old jock who murdered his girlfriend with a tire iron, then claimed his innocence?" She stood, wanting to be able to glare at him eyeball to eyeball. "Or would you like me to tell you about how every prominent donor in this city has called my boss, complaining about some renegade detective snooping into their sex lives." She shook with anger and frustration. "And although Jake didn't say anything to me, I don't doubt those fine, upstanding citizens told him they wouldn't contribute to his upcoming campaign if this investigation continues."

She tried glaring at him; instead tears gathered in her eyes. To her horror, several of them slipped down her cheeks. The harder she tried to stop the moisture, the more they came.

Ash cupped her cheek, making her heart pound and her world shrink to the size of this room. His thumb wiped away the tracks of her tears. Understanding rested in his eyes. "I'm sorry you're getting my fallout."

The warmth of his palm on her face comforted her. "I knew when—"

His thumb slipped down to her lips, stopping her apology.

"Don't." The whispered word fluttered over her lips. "We both know that I sometimes delight in being a rogue."

Her eyes widened at his admission.

He chuckled. "Julie gave me a hard time this afternoon, telling me to behave myself, that we were dealing with rich folks." He shrugged.

Her heart continued to pound. "And your response was?"

"Do you remember when we were dating and that puffed-up little singer tried to intimidate us?"

"You mean that little man at Club Nine?"

He grinned, and she felt it in her stomach. "That's the one."

She remembered the man who was drunk and who'd hit one of his backup singers with a microphone stand. "Yes."

"The little tyrant tried to talk his way out of an assault charge. When I told him I had watched him hit the man, he informed me that the victim deserved what he got. That he was a star and didn't have to put up with a miserable hick criticizing him."

She tried to concentrate on what he was saying, but suddenly all her brain could register was the feel of Ash's thumb running over her mouth, the heat of his big body making the temperature of the room shoot up. "Uh, yeah."

"Well, I got that same reaction today from several people. After the second person torpedoed my question, I got a little more forceful."

She shouldn't be amused, but she was. "How forceful?"

Ash's thumb stilled. He pulled down on her bottom lip, dipping the end of his thumb into the moist backside of her lip. Her knees turned to Jell-O. "I asked direct questions."

She knew she should be more alarmed at what he was saying, but her mind had suddenly gone blank.

"I didn't…beat…around—" with each word he lowered his head until his lips brushed hers "—the bush."

She sighed and melted into his embrace. His mouth covered hers and his arms tightened around her, drawing her flush to his chest. He moved, turning on the desk, setting both feet on the floor. Kelly slid her arms around his chest.

Heaven. And she had missed this paradise so much over the past four years. The melding of their mouths gave as much as it took. He ran the tip of his tongue along the edge of her bottom lip.

He knew how to seduce her and please her. His hand slipped down to her neck, his fingers skimming over her skin. His mouth moved to the corner of hers, then across her cheek. He nipped at the sensitive spot just below her ear. Her head fell back, letting the heat of his mouth wash over her. He worked his way from her ear to under her chin.

She moaned and opened her eyes to stare into his darkened ones. Want and desire arced between them.

A shout of laughter filtered in from the outside office.

They stilled and the world returned with its realities. They were in her office with her co-workers on the other side of that door.

Her arms dropped to her sides. With a smile of regret, he released her. The air between them vibrated with want. And need. His as well as hers.

Kelly stepped away. She took several deep breaths, trying to get control of her racing emotions.

"So, I've ticked off the rich of Houston," he murmured, folding his arms over his large, wonderful chest.

Kelly fought through the sexual haze enveloping her brain. Tearing her eyes away from him, she answered, "You have."

He nodded. "It's good to know I haven't lost my touch."

"You can be assured you haven't." As the words fell between them, their meaning shifted, and suddenly Kelly could only think about sex. Ash had lost none of the animal magnetism he had when they first fell in love.

He stood. "And has your boss shut us down?"

She took a deep breath to steady her nerves. "Uh, no." At this moment, she didn't sound like an intelligent lawyer. She sounded like a lost five-year-old.

Surprise flashed in his eyes. "But what is the caveat in that decision?"

"That you can't go around bludgeoning the upper society of Houston, Ash."

"So how am I going to interview these people?"

"That's what you and I need to decide. We're going to have to come up with a scheme on how you can get information without ticking off these people."

"How?" He stood and walked to the window.

Her nerves were still raw from her encounter with him. "I don't know. Why don't you tell me what you discovered today and we might be able to come up with an idea."

"All right."

Before she could respond, Jake Thorpe walked into her office. He was dressed in a tuxedo. He stared at

Ash, then Kelly. "Good, you're here. We need to talk. In my office now."

Ash and Kelly stared at each other. Their bacon was cooked.

Chapter 7

Ash and Kelly walked into Jake Thorpe's office. When Ash saw Captain Jenkins standing by the window, he knew this meeting wasn't going to be easy. Captain Jenkins wore jeans, T-shirt and running shoes. Obviously, he'd been at home and had been summoned by the D.A. Ash couldn't read the captain's mood, which concerned Ash.

Jake sat at the edge of his desk and nodded for Kelly and Ash to take the seats in front of him.

When they were seated, Jake began, "Let me share with you part of my dinner conversation."

Ash sighed inwardly. He felt Kelly squirm in the chair beside him. Captain Jenkins didn't move from the window.

"I went to a fund-raiser for the mayor. Within five minutes I was cornered by a very angry Samuel Waters. He didn't appreciate his wife's private life being looked into. According to him, what happened in his marriage shouldn't be investigated by the police.''

"She had a brief affair with Andrew Reed," Ash explained. "I wasn't just fishing for who was sleeping with whom."

"I pointed out, Detective, that your questions were related to Catherine Reed's death," Jake answered.

"Didn't that help Mr. Waters to understand?" Kelly asked. "It wasn't as if Ash had a prurient interest in his sex life."

Ash glanced at the woman beside him. Her defense of him warmed him.

"I did. But then Samuel wanted to know why we were still looking into Catherine's death. With her murderer's demise, why wasn't the investigation closed?"

"And did you tell him that this office still has questions?" Kelly asked.

Jake tilted his head and his eyes narrowed. "Remember who you're talking to?"

She flushed.

"I told him. But I had barely turned around when the senior Walter Moen ran straight at me. He informed me that one of my A.D.A.'s was extremely discourteous with him when he questioned her about the status of the Reed case. He didn't appreciate her brusqueness."

Her eyes narrowed. "I'm sure he failed to mention what a pain in the butt he was at that meeting. He also probably didn't mention how he tried to cow me with his position and power. I felt I used a great deal of restraint by not kicking that old goat in the shins."

Jake glanced at Captain Jenkins. "It seems they are perfectly matched."

Jenkins nodded.

The throwaway comment raced through Ash.

"So now, Jake, do you want to stop this investigation?" Kelly asked.

He pinned her with a steel gaze. "No. But Captain Jenkins and I have talked. We think that this case needs to proceed in a different manner."

Jenkins stepped forward. "Ash, if you need your partner to do any work on the Carlson investigation, no problem. But as for Catherine Reed's murder, some changes have to happen."

"Such as?" Ash asked.

"Jake and I have discussed how to proceed without alienating all of Houston's power structure. We want you and Kelly to look into the matter together."

"How's that different from what's happening now?" Kelly asked.

Jake crossed his arms over his chest. "Over the next few months, I have a series of fund-raisers and political events that I need to attend. Most of the people you'll need to interview will be at these events. It will be a perfect time for you, Kelly, to interview them, especially if we downplay the investigation into Catherine Reed's murder."

Kelly's eyes widened and her mouth dropped. "You want me to go to those political mixers?"

"Not only do I want you to go, but I want your date to be Detective Ashcroft."

Ash shot up as if kicked in the butt. "What?" It was amusing to think Kelly had to go to those miserable cocktail-and-smile events. It was quite another for him to be included.

Captain Jenkins moved next to Jake. "We thought it would be natural for you to accompany A.D.A. Whalen. If anyone asks about you two, you can simply play the part of renewed lovers. It will be a touching cover story that you two got back together.''

Ash had the sinking feeling that Captain Jenkins was enjoying this situation a little too much.

''But—'' Kelly started to protest.

''Can you come up with a better cover story, Kelly?'' Jake asked. ''Something that would put these people at ease around you two? If you use the story of reunited lovers, people won't be so wary of you.''

''It depends what they think of their ex's,'' Kelly grumbled.

Ash noticed that Jake swallowed his smile. When he glanced at Captain Jenkins, there was a singleness of purpose in his expression. But a glint of amusement passed through his dark eyes.

''Then I guess we know what we have to do,'' Ash said.

Kelly stared at him, silently asking him if he was okay with this situation. He nodded.

She looked as if she might argue, but after several long moments, she asked, ''When's the first fund-raiser?''

''Day after tomorrow. Dinner at Cattleman's Club. Formal.''

''All right. Ash and I will be there.''

''I think that Ash should go back to the police department. You two can meet privately, away from the D.A.'s office. Set up a place where you can discuss the case and its implications.''

Ash glanced at Kelly. They wanted them to spend time with each other? Alone? What were they up to?

''Then this meeting is over,'' Jake proclaimed. He glanced at his watch. ''I've got a mixer at eight. I'll expect you two to keep me updated daily on what's happening.''

Kelly nodded.

As Ash walked out of the room, he glanced at his boss. Captain Jenkins motioned to him. Ash stopped.

"I assume you don't have a problem with this little setup?" Jenkins said.

It was not a question to which his captain wanted an honest answer. He simply wanted Ash to agree with the decree. "I'm not sure I'm the best detective to throw into these social situations. Julie would be better."

"Julie couldn't go as A.D.A. Whalen's date."

"That's true. It certainly would cause more talk than her bringing her ex-husband. But couldn't Julie go with another detective? She's wonderful at undercover. Remember the work she did at Texas Chic?"

"A.D.A. Whalen's going to need some help. You're it. No one's going to question you two getting back together."

Ash wanted to mutter a few profanities.

"I'll also expect a report from you after every social function on what you gleaned from it and any followups you want to do. I want to be prepared for any nasty calls I get from the citizenry—of which I'm sure there'll be plenty."

This was Captain Jenkins's revenge. "I understand."

"Good."

It was going to be hell. He hated politics, society parties, and having to kiss up to folks he didn't like. When they had been married, Kelly had hauled him to a couple of social functions she had attended. He hadn't liked it.

Added to the already wonderful mix, he had to do this with his ex-wife, pretending that they were an item, again. Of course, after what had just happened in her office…

He didn't want to do this.

He was in trouble.

Ash paced around his apartment, unsettled. This case had suddenly been turned on its head. He was supposed to kiss up to the rich and powerful of the city. Behave himself. Be deferential like some damn servant.

What grated on his sense of fairness was that these people were no different than anyone else in the city. They were murderers, they beat their wives and children, they cheated on their vows, they embezzled from their companies. He loved the idea of catching them with their pants down. But instead of investigating Catherine Reed's murder, he had to play a role of boyfriend to his ex-wife.

But what really threw a kink into this little scenario was that little lip lock he'd experienced with Kelly. Damn, what had inspired such stupidity on his part? When had his common sense taken a walk? When he'd seen the tears in her eyes, that was when. He hadn't been able to stop himself from pulling Kelly into his arms. With her fragrance filling his nose and her body molded to his, Ash had just gone with the flow, dumb as that had proved to be.

His body still hummed with the memory.

He walked into his kitchen and pulled out a ten-year-old bottle of Scotch. He poured a small amount in a glass and downed the fiery liquid.

He found the idea of playing reunited lovers with Kelly before all of Houston society alarming, given what had happened earlier. Just take him out and shoot him and save him from this mess. Not only did he have to fight memories, they were going to have to work together without others to witness their meetings. They would probably have to have daily sessions. And where would they meet? Their house—Kelly's house would be the logical answer.

He remembered how he had pursued her. After their initial coffee date following their class, Kelly had made it clear she wasn't interested in a relationship and he'd backed off. Several months later, he'd been summoned to the chief of police's office to receive an award for helping deliver a baby in the middle of a traffic jam on the Southwest freeway. Kelly had been rushing to work in the chief's office where she worked as PR official, not looking where she was going. They'd literally crashed into each other. Kelly had bounced off him and landed on her rear.

They had both been embarrassed and, while Ash had helped Kelly to her feet, he could've sworn that the floor had shifted beneath his feet. He had returned the next day and asked her out. She hadn't accepted. The next month, at the St. Patrick's Day picnic that the police department held, she'd been there. They had spent the afternoon together. That had been the beginning of a whirlwind courtship. The next six weeks had been the most intense of his life. Every moment he had been off duty, he'd been with her, wanting her.

The phone rang, bringing him out of his memories.

"Ashcroft," he barked into the phone.

There was a pause. "Ash, we didn't get to talk after the meeting with the D.A. and your captain."

Kelly's voice caressed his ears. His mind envisioned her full lips. They belonged on an erotic movie star, not a steel-willed A.D.A. who ate suspects for lunch.

"Yeah."

"Elegant, as ever."

"Kel, I don't need attitude from you. Anyway, I had to get out of there before I let our bosses know how much I don't like being jerked around." He took a deep breath, trying to bring his hormones back into control. "Are you happy having to pretend you're getting back together with your ex-husband?"

The silence on the line unnerved him. He wished he could see her face. She could never lie worth a damn to him. Amazingly enough he could see through the walls that she threw up to keep the rest of the world at bay.

"This isn't any easier for me than you."

Her calm response hit him in the gut. Didn't she have the same reaction to him eating her tonsils as he did to her? Apparently not, and that irritated him.

"Do you still have your tux?" she asked.

"I do. It's in the back of my closet." He'd been tempted to throw it away after the divorce, but reason had argued that he might need it in the future.

"I wanted to check and make sure, since the first party we'll need to attend is day after tomorrow."

"It's clean. I haven't worn it since it came back from the cleaners the last time." *The time when you took it to the cleaners for me.* He didn't say it, but it was understood between them.

"We'll need to talk before then, go over what you found out today." They hadn't had time to discuss what Ash and Julie had discovered in their interviews earlier. Instead, they had spent their time blowing this investigation to smithereens.

"Name the time tomorrow, Kelly. Then we can also float the story that we're closing down the investigation."

"I have court in the morning. Why don't you bring your lunch and we'll do it at noon?"

"Better yet, I'll bring some burgers from Jim's." He wondered why he wanted to bring her favorite food. "It will lend credence to our cover story of starting to date again."

"All right." She paused for a moment, then said, "I know you don't like how things have turned out, but in order to get to the truth in this case, Ash, we're going to have to jump through a few hoops."

"And kiss some a—"

"That doesn't matter. We both believe that Andrew Reed killed his wife."

Her admission blew him away.

They'd never spoken out loud their suspicions about Andrew Reed. It had been understood but never voiced. It shocked him that Kelly willingly stated it aloud.

"Proving it is going to be the challenge." She sighed. "Also, he probably had Carlson killed to cover up his crime. I want to prove it."

"You're right, Kelly. Bringing Andrew Reed to trial for his wife's death is all that matters. I can smile at these society folks, make nice with the rich, to get the proof we need."

"I knew I could count on you."

Her confidence hit him low and hard, jumbling his already confused reactions. "Always, Kelly. Always."

Kelly stared down at the phone in her hand. Confusion clouded her mind. How had she managed to put herself in this hole? Ash's action earlier in her office, holding her, kissing her, comforting her had completely shaken her world. He still knew how she liked to be kissed. That little spot below her ear that always melted her.

She'd been mindless with pleasure when he pulled back. How quickly she'd fallen into that pit of…of…wanting, needing. If he hadn't given her that breather, she would have gladly drowned in that ecstasy.

Her head fell forward. She and Ash were to play the role of reunited lovers. Never in her wildest dreams had she thought she would work with him again—and never, never in this capacity. Captain Jenkins was responsible for this mess. If he hadn't assigned Ash—but he had. And in the end, it was the best choice he could have made.

But wasn't that plan a little too over-the-top? She should just walk into her boss's office and tell him that this wasn't going to work. No one in their right mind would believe she and her ex were getting back together. But hadn't she argued that very point, and Jake had shot her down?

She didn't want to do this. She didn't want to be with Ash, playing that they were in love.

What if she pressed the issue? What reason could she give to her boss? Surely Jake would ask if she still had feelings for Ash. She didn't.

Liar.

And they needed to find a place to discuss this case, away from probing eyes. The logical place would be here at the house. She had a home office.

Her head fell forward in defeat. If she admitted she didn't want to work with him, both Jake and Captain Jenkins would wonder why. She wouldn't be able to hold her head up if they wondered about her reasons. So her only option was to stick this thing out. Smile through gritted teeth and socialize with the upper strata of society.

She gave a snort of laughter. The only person who hated this playacting more than she did was Ash himself. That should be a source of comfort.

During their marriage, when she had a social function to attend and had wanted Ash to accompany her, it was tougher than pulling teeth to convince him to go.

Her mind wandered back to that kiss. She'd melted in his arms, like ice on the hot summer cement. Well, she wouldn't let that happen again. She was over him. She attributed her reaction to the extreme stress of the day. If her boss, or anyone had offered her a shoulder to cry on she would have taken it.

Her reasoning sounded good, but she didn't really believe it for an instant.

Needing to get away from the memories, Kelly stood and walked out of the kitchen.

She still couldn't understand why she'd had that response to Ash. The moment his hand had cupped her cheek, something in her had come back to life, bursting into full bloom.

He still tasted so good.

Wandering down the hall, she stopped in front of the closed door. Her heart clenched. She put her hands on the wood and rested her forehead on it. The baby's nursery.

The pain in her heart wasn't as sharp anymore. She put her hand on the doorknob. After several long moments she turned the handle.

Panic raced over her. She wasn't ready for this. Her hand released the knob. Turning, she strode into her room. That was the closest she'd been to walking into that room since the day Ash closed it after their daughter died.

Kelly went into the bathroom and turned on the

shower, praying she could drown the memories. As she stood under the shower, the water that ran down her cheeks wasn't all from the showerhead.

Ash walked into Homicide. Ralph Lee glanced up from his paperwork.

"I heard the Reed investigation has been put on hold since the main suspect is dead."

"Word gets around quickly," Ash answered.

Ralph shrugged. "I had planned on offering you help now that I'm back from vacation, but I guess it's a moot point."

"Thanks for thinking about me. Funny thing, the case brought a big bonus." Ash would try out their new cover.

"How's that?" Ralph frowned.

Several other detectives had stopped their work and were listening to the exchange. "Well, I've been working with my ex. It seems some things have come together and—well, she and I have decided to try dating again."

Ralph studied him. "You sure you know what you're doing?"

Several of the other detectives laughed. Ash didn't know whether to punch Ralph or agree with him. "Can't say. We all do dumb things."

"Hell, I remember the time I tried dating a lady wrestler," Joe McPherson, Ralph's latest partner, piped in. "She was beautiful, but she could pin me in three seconds flat. I finally got tired of being taken down." He shook his head. "But it was something while it lasted." His smile left none of the other detectives with any doubt as to what the something was.

Ash didn't know whether to be offended or flattered

that his and Kelly's relationship could be compared to Joe's. "Love makes us all look like we're a few bricks short of a full load."

The men laughed.

When Ash approached his partner, he noticed Julie hadn't laughed with the other detectives. Her gaze drilled him.

"What's wrong, partner?" Ash asked.

"You tell me," she quietly replied.

"Why don't you let me buy you a powdered-sugar doughnut at the coffee shop across the street?"

Her gaze searched his. "Sure. I haven't had my sugar and caffeine high this morning. But you're buying."

"No problem."

Julie kept her questions to herself until they were seated in the back of the deserted coffee shop. "So what gives? And don't tell me it's love."

"It could be," he protested good-naturedly.

She didn't look convinced.

"All right. Jenkins and Thorpe jumped all over me and Kelly about my interrogation techniques. I apparently upset several people yesterday."

She nailed him with a glare. "I told you."

"I know, I know. Well, the long and short of it is we're going to float the story that the investigation into Catherine Reed's murder is closed. What Kelly and I plan to do is make the social circuit as a couple, lightly eliciting information. When we develop credible leads, we'll follow up on them.

"You, on the other hand are to take over the investigation into Carlson's murder, be the lead detective. I'll be here, but I'll be working on Catherine Reed's murder. Hopefully this way, we'll be off everyone's radar screen while we learn all their dirty little secrets."

"So love hasn't bitten you on the butt?"

Ash noticed that Julie's gaze didn't waver off his face.

"No," he shot back. The force of his protest made him uncomfortable. "But Kelly and I will have to find a place to meet and discuss the case. So, it's going to look like we're dating. It will be the best cover."

Julie didn't blink. He felt sure she would challenge him on his veracity, but she didn't. She let it slide, much to his relief.

"So you want me to take up the investigation on Carlson's murder."

"I thought that we could do witness interviews today, see what leads we turn up. Then you could do follow-up."

Popping the last of her doughnut into her mouth, she wiped her lips and fingers with a napkin. "Sounds good to me." She studied him. "So you're going to do the social circuit?"

"Yeah." He glared down into his coffee.

"And you feel confident you can do this?"

His head jerked up, stung by his partner's question. "Of course. When Kelly and I were married, I accompanied her to lots of kissy-kissy functions like this. I even have my own tux."

Julie's brow arched. "That's a good attitude."

"I held my own in that shark tank. My problem was I didn't want to be there."

"That must've been pleasant for Kelly."

He remembered a couple of times he had stepped in it big time. He had made it up to Kelly later when they were at home. "There's nothing worse than having to endure a lot of folks trying to impress everyone with how much money they have,'' he answered, trying not to remember those apologies to Kelly.

Julie drained the last of her coffee from the foam cup. "So how's this going to be different?"

"I'll be looking for proof of a couple of murders and not simply socializing."

"So this playacting has purpose for you," she observed. "Dare I suggest you might actually enjoy it?"

He sat back and thought about it from strictly an investigative angle. "You're right."

Julie grinned. She'd been leading him down a path to the see the truth in this situation. He was so close to it, he couldn't look at it logically.

"You really are too smart for your own good," he grumbled good-naturedly.

"I know. Sometimes I'm so clever it kills me."

The note of despair in her voice brought Ash up short. He studied her carefully. Something wasn't right. "What's the problem, Julie?"

"What makes you think anything is wrong?" She tried to bluff him, but he didn't buy it.

"You're talking to your partner. We're honest with each other. I know I've been wrapped up in this investigation and my problems with the department, so I haven't been one hundred percent. What gives?"

"Nothing unusual. Male problems. Had a couple of dates go south. Working in Homicide scares off most men. And one certainly can't talk shop." She shook her head.

They all ran into that problem. Mates and significant others didn't understand that sometimes at the most inopportune moments, you got a call. It had more than one time come at the wrong moment for him and Kelly.

She'd always understood. "You want to unload on me?"

"Naw, I don't want to relive that miserable date." She shook her head. "Let's just say I'm not going to ever date an insurance agent again."

He laughed. "An insurance agent? What ever possessed you do that?"

She shook her head. "A wonderful set of pecs, and don't tell me you haven't dated a woman simply because she was endowed."

He shrugged.

She stood. "Let's go back to work and see what we can discover about Carlson's murder."

Ash and Julie spent the rest of the morning interviewing the residents at the apartment complex where Carlson had lived.

No one had seen anything.

They walked through Carlson's apartment again.

"So if Carlson was murdered, why didn't he put up more of a struggle?" Julie posed the question.

"What if he was surprised by the killer, knocked in the back of the head, then dragged into his bedroom. The killer then staged the murder, placing the gun in Carlson's hand and pulling the trigger. That could account for the odd spray of gunpowder on the victim's hand."

"I like that," Julie agreed.

"What are you doing?" a little voice asked.

Both Ash and Julie turned around to see Sarah Mendoza standing at the door to the bedroom. The four-year-old clutched a well-worn teddy bear to her chest. Her eyes were wide as she studied them.

Ash walked to the little girl and knelt. "We were talking about the other night when Mr. Carlson died."

"Oh." She held her teddy closer and rested her chin on his head. "I didn't like him."

"Who, sweetie," Julie asked.

The little girl solemnly regarded Julie. "The man who yelled at the other man. He scared Teddy." She held up her bear.

"I know." He ran his finger over the bear's head. "Teddy was very brave."

Sarah nodded.

"Have you seen that man around here again since that night?" Ash asked.

"No. But he came before that night."

Ash looked up at Julie. He turned back to Sarah. "That man was here before Mr. Carlson died?"

"He came the day Mr. Carlson moved in." She readjusted her hold on the bear. "They didn't like each other."

"What makes you say that?" Julie asked.

Sarah solemnly looked at Julie. "The scrunchy way Mr. Carlson looked at the other man, kinda like when I hafta eat broccoli."

Ash swallowed a smile. "That bad."

She nodded.

"Did you see that man any other time, Sarah?"

"No."

"Did you ever hear the man's name?"

"No."

"Thank you, Sarah. You have been very helpful." He reached into his sport coat and pulled out a Three Musketeers bar. He held it toward her. "I'd like you to have this."

Delight filled her eyes. "Okay." She grabbed the candy bar and scampered off.

As Ash watched Sarah disappear, he was struck again by the realization that his daughter would have been about her age. He pushed away the painful thought.

"Well, we know that Carlson's killer had been here before the night of the murder." They walked out of the apartment. "I wonder why no one else around there saw him?"

"Or why they don't want to ID the killer," Julie supplied.

"That's what worries me. These folks are afraid of this killer. The question is why." He surveyed the complex, noticing a couple of curtains moving.

The hair on the back of his neck told him he wasn't going to like the answer to his question.

Chapter 8

The smell of burgers from the outside office announced Ash's arrival. Kelly's stomach growled. She glanced down at her watch. Ten minutes to one. He was late and she had to be in court at one-thirty.

"Hey, Ashcroft, you get a second job as a delivery boy?" Curt Richards's voice floated into her office. "If you are, I'm willing to buy one of those burgers."

"Stuff it, Richards," Ash good-naturedly replied.

Laughter filled the air.

"What are you doing here?" Curt asked. "I thought you were finished with the investigation."

"We need to tie up ends. And..." He shaded his reply with innuendo. Although she couldn't see him, Kelly didn't doubt the look of man-to-man conquest exchanged between the males in the other room.

Suddenly Ash filled the doorway, and his size and sexual energy sizzled over her skin. She gritted her teeth against her reaction.

He strolled into her office as if he were on time. "You're lucky I made it through the outer office," he joked. "There were at least three other A.D.A.'s who wanted to buy what I had in the bag." He set the burgers on the edge of her desk. He studied the clutter. "You want to eat in here?"

Thinking about how messy those wonderful burgers were, she shook her head. "Let's go into the conference room." She snatched up the Reed file.

As they walked back across the office, Kelly felt like a suspect in a lineup.

"You sure you don't want to sell those burgers?" Curt Richards questioned again.

Kelly's stomach protested. She stopped and turned to her colleague. "You mess with my lunch, Curt, and I'll charge you with obstructing a law officer in the performance of his duty. If you're hungry, you know where to get a burger."

Curt grinned. "Whoa, you're mean, lady."

"I've got less than forty minutes before I need to be in court."

Ash shrugged. "You know how she is when she's hungry..." He shook his head.

"Tell me about it."

Kelly didn't know who she wanted to smack, Ash or Curt. She settled for glaring at them both, then marched into the conference room.

The instant Ash put the bag on the table, Kelly ripped into it. "Why are you so late?" She hoped he remembered that she had to be in court. Her stomach ached with hunger. It was also a sign of the pressure she felt, her need to eat.

The first bite tasted of heaven. She moaned, enjoying the taste. Ash's choked reaction caused her eyes to flutter open. The heat in his eyes nearly melted her. Suddenly there was a different kind of hunger clawing at her body.

"You always did enjoy your…burgers." The tone of his words held a wealth of meaning that had nothing to do with hamburgers.

She swallowed, tasting nothing.

"Kelly," Teresa Myers walked into the room. "Judge Marks had an emergency and has been called away this afternoon. The trial will resume tomorrow at nine."

"Thanks, Teresa." Kelly glanced at Ash. "Now I don't have to rush back to court and you can explain to me what happened yesterday that caused your boss and mine to go ballistic."

He pulled his burger from the sack. "You know Samuel Waters's wife had an affair with Andrew Reed. Mr. Rich-and-Powerful Waters can wheel and deal land, make bankers jump to his tune, but apparently he doesn't hold that power at home." He took a bite of his burger. "The old man's pride was stepped on by our questioning. He yelled the loudest." He shook his head. "Some rich, old men have very fragile egos. And bluster the likes of which are something to behold."

"Who else did you interview?" she asked around a mouthful of food.

"We talked to the Ackers who held the party the Reeds attended that last night. Talking to them proved to be a gold mine. Mrs. Ackers told us about Andrew being caught with his mistress in front of several witness."

"That wasn't in the file, was it?" she asked, opening and scanning it again for the twentieth time.

"No. Mr. Ackers walked in and shut down the interview. We lucked out when Julie got the name of the mistress from the Ackers housekeeper. Joanna Kris— and Joanna was very bitter about being dumped.'' He went on to explain all they had learned at the interview. ''Joanna was downing tequila as if it was going out of style when we interviewed her. She talked pretty freely.''

He paused, and Kelly knew something wrong had occurred. When he glanced at her, all her instincts confirmed her fears.

''Tell me the rest, Ash. What went wrong?''

He rubbed his chin. ''Joanna was very helpful for the first part of the interview.''

Kelly went still. ''The first part. What about the second part?''

''She suddenly clammed up on us. She was talking, venting about what a miserable money-grubbing bastard Andrew Reed was, then she quit. And neither Julie or I could figure out why.''

''Run it by me,'' Kelly offered.

''Julie's going to write up the interview. I'll get it when I go back to HPD headquarters this afternoon, then we can review it. But Joanna did tell us that Andrew Reed's new fiancée is loaded.''

''And Joanna isn't?''

''Apparently not. She married and divorced money but didn't have any of her own and that puts her as a mistress, not a wife.''

''But I thought Andrew Reed was well off.''

Ash tapped his fingers on the table. ''It adds a whole new dimension to this investigation.''

''Yes. We're going to need to do some financial reviews.''

No wonder all those society folks screamed to high

heaven about being interviewed. People in their tax bracket usually didn't get interviewed by homicide cops about a murder among their own. Or get audited. It made them uncomfortable. It pulled back the veneer of sophistication to reveal the darker side of their existence.

Kelly popped another French fry into her mouth. "Tonight is the first party we're scheduled to attend at the Cattleman's Club."

"What time?"

"Cocktails are at seven. I'll meet you there."

He stilled, his eyes dark, unreadable, and a muscle in his jaw flexed. "I don't think so."

He took her breath away. "What are you talking about?" she asked, ignoring her reaction.

"We're an item, remember?"

"As if I could forget."

That earned her a glare. "If we arrive in separate cars, no one is going to buy our cover story. I'll pick you up."

Kelly wanted to avoid that. It would resemble a date, which was something she wanted to avoid. She opened her mouth, then shut it. Common sense told her Ash had a valid point.

"Good." Satisfaction settled in his eyes. "I'll be at your house at six forty-five."

There was no way around it. "Fine."

"Don't act like you're going to your execution. If anyone should act that way, it's me. You know how I hate fund-raisers."

That wasn't all that bothered him. She didn't doubt he hated playing the role of her boyfriend. "I'll see you then."

After he left the room, Kelly rested her head on her

arms. She didn't want to do this, didn't want to pretend to be infatuated with Ash. She didn't want to play interested girlfriend, because it brought back too many memories that she didn't want to recall.

At six forty-five Ash pulled his car into the driveway of his old house. As if this situation wasn't bizarre enough, he felt as if he were coming home. The honeysuckle bush blooming under the living room window filled the air with its sweet fragrance. He remembered making love to Kelly with that scent filling his nostrils.

His mind shied from the memory. He was here strictly as a cop, doing undercover, per instructions of his boss. Nothing else.

Sure, a little voice in his head whispered. *And it snows in Houston.*

It did snow in Houston, he assured himself. Maybe only once in fifty years, but it happened.

He slid out of his car and walked to the door. When he rang the bell, the door instantly opened. Kelly's shape was silhouetted by the light behind her. The simple black dress she wore faithfully outlined her curves. She was a size ten, liked satin underthings, and didn't own a single white bra or panties. When he asked about that, she explained that, when she was growing up in Beaumont, her parents didn't have enough money to buy anything fancy for their daughter. Plain white cotton. After her father died in an accident, there had been even less. Once she had earned enough, she never again bought white or cotton underthings.

The wind danced around Kelly, moving her shoulder-length hair. This was the first time he'd seen it down. She'd let it grow.

Desire nearly brought him to his knees.

He was here for a job and nothing more, dammit.

Her eyes roamed over him, intimately. "You look very nice."

Mercy, Kel.

He tugged at the neck of his shirt. "I'd rather be in a T-shirt and jeans."

"Of that I have no doubt." She pulled the lacy shawl over her shoulders and stepped out into the night air.

She wore high heels that showed off her legs to their best advantage.

Why not just take him out and shoot him and put him out of his misery?

"I tried to get a list of who was invited to this event. There are going to be several couples who were at the party where Catherine was killed."

She walked around the car to the passenger door. Ash followed and opened the door for her. She threw him a questioning look.

"I thought I'd play this part so no one can claim we're just going through the motions."

She glanced around the yard. "I don't see anyone."

"Better to cover ourselves. We can't see what neighbors are watching, and you know Mrs. Schattle likes to gossip."

Their eighty-year-old neighbor knew all the comings and goings on the street and discussed it with anyone who'd listen to her.

Kelly nodded and slid into the front seat. As Ash walked around the car, he reminded himself of what the object of this evening was.

Kelly picked up the file folder on the seat. "What's this?"

"A copy of the report Julie wrote of our interview with Joanna Kris."

She opened the folder and tried to read it, but with the light quickly disappearing, she closed it. "I'll read it later."

She glanced around the Jeep. "I'm surprised you're not still driving your truck."

He'd been so proud of that Ford. It was the first vehicle he'd bought after he had graduated from high school. He'd been very possessive of his truck and hadn't even allowed his mother or sister to drive it. When he had tossed the keys to Kelly and told her to take it to run an errand, his sister had announced her brother must be in love.

"It was stolen by some teens in my apartment complex and totaled." He had been madder than hell when he'd discovered what had happened. "It was amusing to see their reactions when they realized they'd stolen a cop's truck."

"I bet you gave them a rough time."

"You bet I did."

She shook her head. "Why don't we run over the guest list and see who we need to talk to."

"Okay," Ash mumbled.

And someone better talk, because he was paying a mighty high price for this information.

Kelly glanced around the crowded room. Diamonds, emeralds, sapphires and rubies sparkled off every female who walked through the door. It seemed to be a contest as to who had the biggest, costliest necklace, bracelet or ring. Or the oldest husband.

"There's not a sensible wealthy man in this city, is there?" Ash muttered.

Kelly stared up at him. He stood next to her, his arm around her waist. It was hard to concentrate on anything besides his heat and the feel of his large hand on her waist. He had been closer that a kick-a-ber on her old hound since they'd walked into this shindig. And they had raised several eyebrows.

A choked laugh came from her throat.

Ash threw her a knowing look. "I wasn't the only one thinking that, was I?"

"No. But I feel out of place without any high-priced jewelry."

His gaze roamed over her neck and upper breasts. "There's nothing wrong with what you have on."

"I feel naked," she whispered.

His gaze slid over her body very slowly, telling her that he didn't take her comment in the same vein she offered it. The corner of his mouth turned up and he leaned down and whispered, "You would definitely stand out."

In his eyes, she could see him remembering exactly what she looked like clothed only in skin.

She swallowed, hard. "Jewelry," she croaked.

"Ah." A wealth of meaning filled that simple sound. He'd nearly knocked her socks off when he had shown up at her door this evening. The tux gave him an air of dangerous male, barely tamed by the constraints of civilization. The way he had looked at her made her mind go blank and her blood heat. She felt like a high-school girl with her first crush. This was no way for an A.D.A. to behave.

"Relax." His fingers tucked a strand of hair behind her ear.

Fire from his touch sizzled along her nerves.

"Everyone knows that you're with the D.A.'s office." His fingers pushed aside her bangs. "If you had on something very expensive, they'd be yelling that their taxes were being spent the wrong way."

Her mind groped for a coherent answer. Stop it, she ordered. She was a grown woman. An A.D.A., so she needed to act like it. "Or that I'm on the take," she grumbled.

"Or it could be you've acquired a wealthy boyfriend," he added.

"Nope, Ash, that story won't work, now. You're it and you better not be making the kind of money that could provide me with something like that."

He shrugged. "One of the disadvantages of dating a cop." His hand settled on the sensitive skin at the back of her neck, nearly making her jump out of her skin.

She looked at him. Her skin tingled where his hand rested. "What are you doing?" she hissed.

He bowed his head, his mouth next to her ear. "I'm playing the part that the D.A. has assigned to me. We've rediscovered each other. If I don't act interested, communicate with body language that you and I are an item, I doubt anyone will buy our story."

The look he gave her betrayed his words, nearly melting her knees. He wasn't as unaffected as he would have her believe.

"Maybe you could turn the act down a few notches," she answered.

"Depends."

"On what?"

"If you want Walter Moen to believe our cover story."

"Wal—"

Ash pulled her close and brushed her lips with a light kiss. "The enemy is twelve o'clock behind you," he whispered against her mouth.

Yanking hard on her self-control, she pulled back and stepped to Ash's side, then scanned the crowd. Walter Moen stood near the bar, glaring at them. He walked toward her. She stiffened.

"Easy, Counselor," he breathed. His hand settled on the small of her back.

Walter stopped in front of them. "I was very glad to learn the investigation into Catherine Reed's murder has been discontinued."

Kelly forced a smile. "I'm sure you were." Ash's hand tightened on her waist.

Walter nodded. "Her parents were very glad to hear that information, too. Nothing would have come of continuing to look into that tragedy."

Except the truth. Kelly swallowed her response.

"The D.A. agreed with my position when I talked to him," Walter forged on. He was drunk enough not to be reading her signals clearly.

Kelly remained silent. After an awkward moment, Walter nodded and walked off.

"Old goat," she grumbled.

Ash laughed, a deep, stirring sound. He leaned down and placed his mouth next to ear. "He is a bit prissy."

She shook her head. "You're encouraging me in bad thoughts."

"Naw, I'm just confirming that your instincts are right on the mark. And I'm proud that you didn't let the SOB have it between the eyes." He hadn't backed up an inch, his body pressed against hers.

"You know me too well."

Her comment made them both aware how intimately they knew each other, their strengths and weaknesses. Their bodies fit together with remembered ease.

Kelly squared her shoulders. "We better start working the room to see if we can discover any whispers about the Reed marriage. We probably have a half hour to mingle before dinner.''

Ash nodded and started through the crowd. He smiled at several couples as he walked to the bar.

"Give me a whiskey," he told the bartender. He wouldn't drink it, but it would be good window dressing.

What was happening to him, to be flirting with Kelly like that? Had he lost all his sense? Where was his sense of self-preservation? His captain was just getting back at him by putting him through this torture.

As he moved through the crowd, he heard snatches of conversation drifting to him.

"...and Karen discovered Jim red-handed with his secretary..."

"...the trip to Paris only took four hours on the Concord..."

"...she won a scholarship to Rice..."

"...glad that messiness about Catherine is ended. I thought..."

He paused, intrigued with the conversation.

"Hello, there." The greeting had a breathy quality.

Ash turned to the very well endowed blonde. She had a killer look in her eyes. She was fishing for a conquest and he looked like the next victim.

"Hello," he answered.

"Are you alone?" the woman asked, moving in for the kill. Her perfume penetrated the air. Her tongue came out and wet the corner of her collagen-enhanced lips. That probably wasn't the only thing that was enhanced.

"No." He held out his hand. "Tony Ashcroft."

She caressed his hand. "I'm Tanya Summers."

When she released his hand, Ash was tempted to glance down and make sure he still had all his fingers. "Are you here by yourself, Tanya?"

"No. My husband's over there by the bar."

Ash glanced to where she pointed. Standing by the bar were two men. One was in his sixties. The other was in his mid-thirties. Just then, the older man turned and nodded to Tanya.

She smiled at her husband and waved. When she turned back to Ash, she carefully studied him. "I'm his third wife."

Ash nodded. "How long have you been married?"

"We just celebrated our third anniversary. He flew me to Switzerland. It took my breath away. Those lovely banks have such a wonderful system."

If nothing else, Tanya was honest. He smiled.

She touched his arm. "And who are you here with?"

Ash pointed to Kelly, who was talking to an older woman. "That's my date, Kelly Whalen."

Tanya looked coyly at him, her fingers walking up his arm. "And what does she do?"

"She's an assistant district attorney."

Her eyes widened. "Why would you want to date someone like that?"

"Because I'm a cop." Ash leaned closer. "And isn't this a fund-raiser for the current D.A.?"

Tanya shrugged off the logic. "It's a party my husband wanted to come to. I don't pay attention. I just enjoy." She glanced at Kelly again and frowned. "Isn't she the one who was involved with that big murder—uh—Catherine Reed? Wasn't she the prosecutor?"

Tanya wasn't as dumb as she appeared. The woman knew what was happening in this city. "Yes."

She studied him, then Kelly. "So you like smart women?"

"Guilty."

She bit her bottom lip. She was a good actress. "That's such a shame." When he frowned, she added, "Cat's murder."

"I heard that her husband was running around on her," Ash confided.

She pulled back and stared at him. "I don't doubt that."

"Why do you say that?"

"Because the old boy cheated on his mistress with the current female he's engaged to." She leaned closer. "It's rumored that the upcoming Mrs. Reed has more money than his last wife."

"I hadn't heard that."

"Then you don't have your ear to the ground. Her daddy was one of the founders of the software giant, Pegasus."

"But what about the woman he was involved with before. Why didn't he marry her?"

Tanya's brow arched. "She was good in the sack, but she was broke. She's the kind you enjoy but don't marry."

Ash glanced at Tanya.

"I'm in a different boat. My hubby had the money." She sighed. "I don't think Andrew Reed ever forgot who had the purse strings in his marriage. Rumor was that Catherine wanted a divorce. Her death came at the right time for Andrew."

"It sure sounds like it."

She studied Ash. "What kind of cop are you?"

"I'm a detective."

"Doing what?"

"Investigating."

Rubbing her chin, her gaze roamed over his face. "You're not interested in a little entertainment, are you?" Tanya asked.

"Cops tend to be square, Tanya."

She shook her head. "That's a shame."

He nodded toward Kelly. "She doesn't think so."

Tanya glanced over her shoulder at Kelly. She turned back to him. "I hope she knows what a winner she has." She took a step away, then stopped. "If you change you mind, you can find me at Houstonian Club working out every day at ten in the morning."

"I'll remember that."

"Do." The invitation rang clearly.

The sponsor of the fund-raiser, the wife of the owner of the largest car dealership in the city, stepped to the microphone. "Dinner is ready. After we eat, there will be dancing. And please be sure to meet our D.A. and open your checkbooks and give."

The crowd moved toward the dining room. Ash slipped in beside Kelly. She glanced up at him.

"I hope that conversation netted some good information," she quietly commented as they walked.

He shook his head. "You sound jealous."

"She was all over you. I'm surprised she didn't drag you off into the bushes."

A laugh rumbled in his chest. "She offered, but I told her I was with you."

Kelly didn't look amused.

Ash pulled her arm through his. "But she gave me a gold mine of information."

"That's not all she gave you."

Tanya and her husband filed into the dining room before them.

"I'm surprised her husband doesn't drag her home and start divorce proceedings," Kelly grumbled.

Ash shook his head. "Not in a million years. That man parades Tanya around in front of his friends, showing off his ability to get a young, beautiful woman."

"And it doesn't bother him that all she's interested in is his bank account?"

"There are compensations."

"No, Ash, there aren't." The militant look in her eyes told Ash it would be useless to argue. Oddly enough, he didn't want to. She had a point.

"I think that went very well," Ash murmured in Kelly's ear as they swayed to the slow song the band played.

She looked up. Dinner had been hell as far as she was concerned. "What makes you think so?"

"You didn't jump down Samuel Waters's throat when he said he was relieved that all that nonsense about Catherine's death had ceased." His eyes twinkled.

"The only reason I didn't say anything is because that fine gentleman was one of the loudest protesters against the investigation." Ash's gaze captured hers. "Maybe you ought to look into his relationship with Andrew and Catherine Reed."

"You don't think there was something—"

"No." She shook her head. "I don't think that. But it seems to me there's something else driving that old man."

"What's driving him is his wife had an affair with Andrew Reed."

She jerked back and met his gaze. "How do you know?"

"I heard it while I was in the crowd. I also learned something very important from the lady who was friendly with me earlier."

"What was that?"

"That the reason Andrew Reed dropped his old mistress was because he caught a new woman who has money. And apparently Catherine Reed didn't like her husband fooling around on her and was going to divorce him."

A light clicked on in Kelly's gaze. "And Catherine was the one with money, wasn't she?"

"Apparently, from what Tanya said. It appears that Andrew Reed's background needs to be looked into."

"So, if you checked with Catherine's personal lawyer, you might discover whether she'd talked about a divorce."

"I can do that."

"You turned up a gold mine, Ash."

"I don't know, but we'll soon see."

Chapter 9

Ash tried to survey the crowd as he danced with Kelly, but it was impossible with her head tucked against his shoulder. He pulled her lush body closer and felt his own respond.

"What are you doing?" she whispered harshly into his neck.

Her warm breath on his skin only added to his misery, but in spite of his hormones, he heard the irritation in her voice. Her hand, hidden by his tux jacket, slid to his side and pinched. They might look like lovers, but from her reaction, she wasn't going along with the plan.

"I'm trying to study everyone in the room. I want to see their reactions, see if anyone is glaring at us or fuming." He pulled back and gave her a smile filled with hot passion.

Her eyes widened, her lips parted and he felt the fine ripple that raced through her body.

"What—"

He leaned his head down and whispered, "Andrew Reed just walked into the reception with the next Mrs. Reed."

Kelly stiffened. Ash didn't relax his hold, but continued moving to the old Righteous Brothers' song. "Is he looking?"

He rubbed his chin on the top of her head. "He's looking, murder in his eyes."

"It won't be the first time," Kelly whispered.

Ash looked down at her and grinned. "The fiancée went one direction, and he's moving toward the dance floor."

The music about endless love swirled around them.

"Ah, he's stopped and is talking to a group of men, Walter Moen among them."

The song ended. Ash pulled back. "You ready for this performance?"

She returned his sultry look. "I am." She started toward the men.

Andrew turned and stepped forward as Ash and Kelly walked by his table. "Good evening, Detective Ashcroft." He nodded to Kelly. "Ms. Whalen."

They returned his greeting, then acknowledged the other men standing with Andrew. Walter Moen glared at Kelly. She calmly smiled at him. A spurt of pride raced through Ash.

Andrew looked down his nose at them. "I'm surprised to find you at this fund-raiser."

"Aren't members of the D.A.'s office allowed to come to these events?" Kelly answered.

"Of course. Are you going to contribute?"

Kelly smiled but didn't answer the rude question.

Andrew's gaze moved to Ash. "And does the police department also send representatives?"

"I'm Kelly's date," Ash supplied.

Andrew frowned. "But weren't you two—uh—divorced?" He looked at the crowd around them for support. "That's what I heard."

Kelly drew herself up and Ash knew she was fixing to let the miserable little toad have it. They couldn't afford to blow their cover at this point of the investigation.

Ash slipped his arm around Kelly's waist and drew her flush against his side. His hand tightened on her hip. "There was an unexpected benefit that came with the Carlson investigation."

Andrew stiffened. Ash had hit the mark.

"Since Kelly and I had to work together again, it sparked old feelings, and—" He looked down at her with an expression that he hoped resembled love. She smiled back. He didn't know if she fooled the crowd, but his body believed her. He turned back to the audience. "And we're seeing each other again."

"Congratulations," Andrew muttered through stiff lips.

The other men in the group offered their good wishes.

"Where's your fiancée?" Ash asked.

"Michelle's in the powder room," Andrew explained.

After a brief, uncomfortable moment, Ash excused them and they walked to their table.

"He's a miserable human being," Kelly grumbled.

Ash laughed and leaned close. "Careful, Counselor, your bias is showing."

Fire flared in her eyes, then the corner of her mouth turned up. "Quit jerking my chain."

"I thought I'd warn you. We've made some amazing

progress tonight. We want to keep the image up and
see what other leads we can uncover.''

Kelly gathered her dignity. ''All right. Let me make
a visit to the powder room before we leave. Since the
future Mrs. Reed went in that direction, maybe I can
corner her and have a chat.''

She moved through the crowd, grateful to escape the
fishbowl atmosphere of the reception. The hall to the
powder room was blessedly quiet. She walked into the
elegant room and the woman who was powdering
her face stopped. She stared at Kelly in the mirror.

''Why are you after my fiancé?'' Michelle Graham,
who couldn't be more than twenty-five, demanded.

So much for having to come up with an excuse to
talk to her. ''Are you talking to me?'' Kelly asked.

Michelle turned and her eyes narrowed. ''Why do
you want to continue to make Andrew's life miserable?
He lost his wife. Wasn't that enough?''

''The D.A.'s office isn't after Mr. Reed. There were
just some matters that had to be cleaned up after the
state supreme court overturned Carlson's conviction.''

''Well, he's dead now, isn't he?''

So much for a kind and sympathetic response. ''Yes,
he is.''

''Then all this should be going away and it's about
time. Andrew and I are to be married in two weeks. A
big church wedding and this—this mess has ruined everything. The talk at my showers and dinners is only
about how awful it is that man got out of prison.''

''How has Andrew been since the news?'' Kelly
asked, hoping for an insight into the man.

''How do you think he's been? Upset and distracted.
Talking to his lawyers. Talking to the police. Numerous
time. We haven't made—'' She glared at Kelly as if it

were her fault for the status of Michelle's love life. "I'm so glad it's over."

Apparently Michelle didn't see beyond herself. "I wish you well," Kelly offered.

The woman nodded, put her compact in her purse and walked out of the room.

Kelly breathed deeply. She quickly took care of her needs, washed her hands, then walked back into the reception. Glancing around, she found Michelle hanging on Andrew's arm.

Ash appeared at Kelly's side, her shawl in his hand. "What happened?" he asked, settling the light fabric around her shoulders.

"I didn't have to work too hard to engage Andrew Reed's fiancée. She came at me with both barrels." She nodded to the woman.

He looked at the couple across the room. "She came at you?"

Kelly slipped her arm through his and started toward the door. "Let's go home."

The word *home* gave her pause, but he didn't behave as if he were waylaid by her comment.

They didn't speak again until they were driving away.

"What happened with Michelle Graham?"

"Michelle is upset that our investigation is screwing up her marriage plans. Clouding the magic of the time. How can you enjoy being the center of attention, your every whim catered to, when your fiancé is being asked about the brutal slaying of his last wife?"

Kelly took a deep breath. "Maybe she wasn't that crass, but she wanted to know when it was going to stop. The Texas Supreme Court mucked up her wedding. And her love life."

"What did you tell her?" Amusement laced his voice.

"This isn't funny, Ash." Kelly folded her arms over her chest.

"No, it isn't. It's just that I find it fascinating the little girl jumped you."

Kelly laid her head on the seat back. "I wanted to tell her that she didn't want to get hitched to that monster. Didn't she know what a two-timing bastard he was." She rolled her head to the side to see his reaction.

A broad smile curved his mouth. A mouth that had been so close while they were dancing. A mouth that seduced and beckoned. If she wasn't careful, she would find herself in a world of hurt.

"Of course, Carlson's death solved all her problems. And she didn't seem that broken up about his demise."

"Did you expect she would?"

It was an ugly truth. "No."

"Good, a realistic answer. I intend to investigate Michelle's financial status tomorrow. And Andrew's."

"I'll be in court tomorrow morning, but let me know what you uncover."

He pulled up into the driveway of her house. Kelly didn't wait for him to come around and open the door. Instantly she grabbed the file he'd given her earlier and opened the car door. She met him in front of the car.

"You should've waited," he quietly reproved.

She didn't answer him. He pulled her arm through his. She hesitated.

"C'mon, Kel, let's see this thing through. Mrs. Schattle is watching."

She prayed the older woman wasn't using her binoculars, because she'd see Kelly's rebellious expression. After a long moment, she nodded and allowed him to walk her to the door, knowing it would look suspicious if he didn't.

She paused after she unlocked the door, and looked into his face. From the shadows cast by the porch light, she couldn't see his eyes.

"Why don't we step inside for a moment? We want to leave Mrs. Schattle to wonder about whether I give you a good-night kiss, that is unless you want me to give you one in front of her and all the neighbors?"

"Inside."

"I thought so."

He quietly walked in behind her, then closed the door.

"How long do you suppose I should wait?"

"Since this is the first time she's seen us together, a couple of minutes is all."

His solemn gaze met hers.

"I'll read over the file you gave me."

"We need a place where we can meet on a regular basis to work on the case—somewhere out of the public eye." He glanced into the living room. There was an office just off that room.

There was no help for it. The office here in the house was the most logical place for them to meet. It would also give them cover. To the outside world, it would look like he was coming to spend time with her and the romantic angle would explain his presence.

"We can use the office here."

He met her gaze. The world stopped. Fire blazed in his eyes, melting her. But neither one of them moved. There seemed to be some sort of force field that held them in place.

A thousand wants and wishes assailed her. But they were wishes that couldn't be granted.

Finally he reached out. Then his hand stopped inches from her face and dropped to his side.

"I'd better leave."

That was the right thing to do.

He quietly slipped out of the door.

She locked it behind him, praying this would get easier, because, up to now, it hadn't.

Ash stared at the ceiling. The moonlight pouring through the windows bathed the rough surface with shadows and mystery. He remembered the night he and Kelly had counted the cracks in the ceiling of their bedroom. They'd replastered the next weekend he had off.

Shit. Why was everything suddenly a memory of something they had done together as a couple?

"Because, fool, until you solve this case you're going to be with her," he muttered into the darkness. And the sad fact was, at the rate he was going, things were going to get rough.

The divorce had been the right thing to do. After Kelly had miscarried, they hadn't been able to talk. Every time he tried to hold her, comfort her, she would pull away. She'd buried herself in work.

The miscarriage had hurt him, too, but there didn't seem to be any words he could say that would help. Instead, he had also turned to his work. As the days passed, they didn't talk. Didn't touch. Didn't make love.

When Kelly had announced that she thought they should divorce, it had been easier just to go along with the plan. It was the coward's way, but he hadn't been ready to deal with that issue, himself.

Suddenly this miserable case was bringing up all those problems that hadn't been resolved. So now what did he want to do? Every time he touched Kelly, he wanted to pull her into a dark corner and explore the magic that they knew, and heaven knows he'd had his hands all over her last night.

Ash glanced at the clock on the nightstand. Three-twenty.

He could stay in bed, rehash the other things that had gone wrong in his marriage or think about how Kelly felt in his arms. Or he could get out of bed and go to police headquarters and use the department computers to see if he could come up with any leads. There wasn't any contest.

He quickly dressed and drove downtown. A few detectives were in at their desks.

"Hey, Ash, what are you doing here this time of the night?" Barry Forbes asked.

"I couldn't sleep. A case was bothering me, so..."

Barry nodded. "I know. Had a case like that last year."

He grabbed a cup of coffee, then sat down at his desk and started looking into the financial status of Andrew Reed and his fiancée, Michelle Graham. He also had to write up a summary of what had happened last night at the fund-raiser.

He lost himself in the work.

"You look like hell."

Julie's cheerful observation stopped him. He looked up and saw that most of the detectives for the day shift were here.

"Thanks, partner. I'm glad to know you don't hold back your observations."

"You don't want girl observations out of me. You want cop."

He grunted.

"So the date went that well?" she quietly asked.

Seeing the warning in her eyes, he glanced around the room. Ralph Lee and his partner had paused, listening.

Ash leaned back in his chair. "You know how chichi functions are. The more money you got, the more you have to show it off. Money was on parade last night. Enough diamonds to choke a horse."

"Well, we know that nothing disastrous happened," Julie added, "because we would've heard about it on the evening news."

"You're not talking to the right folks. You need to ask people like my neighbor, Mrs. Schattle. They know all about what's going on in their neighborhood."

Captain Jenkins walked through the room. "Ashcroft, in my office."

Julie gave Ash a sympathetic smile. Ash grabbed the report he'd finished and walked into Captain Jenkins's office. He closed the door behind him and handed the report to his captain.

Jenkins scanned the sheet. "So, you're looking into Andrew Reed's financial records."

"And the fiancée, after she jumped on Kelly in the ladies' bathroom."

"And you thought this would be a miserable assignment with no action."

Breaking up catfights wasn't high on his list. Nor was having to keep his arms around his ex-wife. He felt as if he were at the top of a hill and everyone behind him was pushing. "I also want to meet with Catherine Reed's lawyer to see if she ever talked to him about a divorce."

"From this report, it sounds like you've turned up several solid leads. Let me know how it pans out."

Ash stared at Jenkins. "That's it?"

He looked up from his paperwork. "What were you expecting?"

"After the decree the other day, I expected an interrogation on every bigwig we talked to."

Captain Jenkins gave him a don't-be-a-jerk look. "In spite of recent evidence, you know how to behave yourself. I'm sure the A.D.A. wouldn't have let you get out of line."

That was it?

"You have several leads to track down, Detective," Jenkins said in a no-nonsense matter.

"I'll need my partner."

"So?"

Ash knew when he was defeated. He opened the door.

"I'll expect to be updated after the next fund-raiser, and also if you turn up any more interesting leads."

Ash didn't see a need to respond. He walked to his desk. "C'mon, partner, I'm going to need some help."

As they made their way down to the garage, he said, "Who was a close friend of Catherine Reed?"

"I'm not sure. She was a member of the Houston Arboretum."

"Arboretum? As in plants?"

"Sure." Julie smiled. "A lot of rich ladies are members."

"Then we're going to look at plants and see if we can find a friend of Catherine Reed."

Kelly welcomed the workload. With the high-school jock found guilty and the trial over, she'd been assigned another two cases. Depositions, witnesses to interview and prepare. Maybe she could get pleas from the defendants.

"Kelly, I want to talk to you." Jake Thorpe strolled into her office and sat on the corner of her desk. "You and Ash made quite an impression at the fund-raiser last night."

She didn't want to think about it. She hadn't fallen asleep until the wee hours of the morning, then she'd overslept and was late for court. "I'm glad."

"I've had several people stop me, telling me how impressed they were with you and Ash, asking when you two were getting married."

She gaped at him. "What?"

"The act you two put on was very good. You even had me believing that there was something going on between you two. I had a couple of ladies, who'd expressed dismay over the Reed investigation, tell me how romantic they found your story."

She didn't want to hear that. "What can I say? We're good."

"And I heard that you turned up several good leads," he added.

"From whom?"

"Captain Jenkins called me. He also was pleased with Ash's report. He's out chasing down those sources." He stood. "Our next event is tomorrow night. This one is a barbecue. If you've got western, wear it."

Kelly stared at the doorway. Jake had breezed in, told her "good job," and breezed out as if nothing had happened. She felt as if the world had exploded and nothing was the way it had been before Ash had walked back into her life.

She worked for another two hours to prepare for tomorrow before driving home.

When she pulled into her driveway, Ash's car was parked there. He sat on her porch in the old wooden rocker.

Her battered heart nearly stopped. She didn't want to deal with him. Not now. She got out of her car and slowly walked up to the front door. "I wasn't expecting you."

"I thought you might like to know what I uncovered today."

He had a point. "Is Mrs. Schattle watching?"

"She's there." He smiled and stood. Kelly walked into his arms.

She meant to keep the kiss brief, perfunctory, a show for their audience. But the instant she felt his lips on hers, her mind went blank. Suddenly the lousy day disappeared in the onslaught of heat and excitement.

His arms slipped around her back and he pulled her close. The warmth and strength of his body seeped into her being, a welcome relief. Her briefcase slipped out of her hand, landing with a loud thud, and she grabbed on to the back of his shirt. His tongue demanded entrance to her mouth. She eagerly opened, tasting the unique quality that was Ash.

His hand spread wide on the small of her back and he fit her into the contours of his body. He nibbled at the corner of her mouth, then rested his forehead against hers.

He pulled back and smiled at her. "I think we've probably given Mrs. Schattle enough to talk about."

Reality slapped her. This was an act.

She stepped away, picked up her briefcase and unlocked the front door. He followed her down the hall into the kitchen. She put her briefcase on the table and turned to face him. There wasn't a gloating expression on his face, but one of understanding.

"What did you learn?"

He moved into the room and pulled out chair and sat. "We found a friend of Catherine's at the arboretum. An old high-school friend. She explained that, several months before her death, Catherine had told her she intended to divorce her husband. She'd gone to her old family lawyer to discuss the plan."

"You got a name? And did she see this lawyer?"

"Yes and yes." He grinned, obviously relishing holding back the information.

"Am I supposed to psychically know what was said or are you going to tell me?"

"Catherine's old family lawyer was Dean Ricker. She had asked him four months before her death to start divorce proceedings. She called him back two weeks later and told him she'd changed her mind."

"Didn't he think the cops needed to know this information?" Kelly asked.

"Mr. Ricker had a stroke a month before Catherine's death. He was still in the hospital when she was murdered. Once he recovered, he didn't see a need to bring up the subject since a man had been convicted for Catherine's murder."

Kelly leaned back against the cabinets. "What do you want to bet that Andrew Reed breathed a whole lot better knowing Dean Ricker had had a stroke."

Ash stood and moved to her side. "You're wondering if Andrew had anything to do with that stroke."

After a moment of stunned amazement, she laughed. "How did you know?"

"I know how your mind works." *And I know a lot of other things that you like.*

He didn't say it, but Kelly read it in his eyes.

Her stomach rumbled, breaking into the tension of the moment. "You hungry?"

"Yeah."

"Let me change, then we can get something to eat and discuss what else you discovered today. I also wanted to go over the Reed file again, to see if we've missed anything."

"You got it."

Kelly walked into her bedroom, trying to still her racing heart. She rested both her hands on the dresser and took a deep, steadying breath. To come home to see Ash waiting for her pierced her with longing and sweet memories.

When she'd kissed him, only because Mrs. Schattle was watching, she assured herself, it completely knocked her senseless.

"Get hold of yourself, Kelly Whalen," she whispered. "You're beyond this. Act like it." She threw back her head and looked into the mirror.

She could do this. And she had to remember that Ash's actions out there on the porch had been simply for show.

You're lying, a voice inside her head whispered.

She might be, but it was the only way she was going to survive.

Chapter 10

Ash moved closer to Kelly as she pointed to a notation in the original file of the Reed murder investigation. Their dinner had been fajitas and black beans at a small Mexican restaurant around the corner.

"It says that Andrew claimed he went to the Coffee Cup after he dropped his wife off, but—" She turned to him, her mouth inches from his. Their gazes locked.

Ash fought his instincts. He'd stepped over the line earlier tonight when they gave the performance for Mrs. Schattle. He determined not to do that again. He was here only because they wanted to find the evidence to catch Catherine Reed's murderer.

"Yes?"

She swallowed. "Uh, his alibi was never checked out."

He looked down at the file. He thumbed through the different pages and reports. "You're right. There was never a follow-up."

"And why do you suppose that is?"

"Maybe Ralph didn't think he needed to once they caught Carlson." He wouldn't have let that point slip, but he wanted to give the other detective the benefit of the doubt. "I've been sloppy."

"No. Not like that. You, Ash, are a royal pain, going off on tangents, doing things that make the D.A.'s office crazy, but you don't leave loose ends dangling like that, especially since Andrew was a suspect." She pushed away from the desk, stood and paced. "You said yourself that this crime was one of passion—no, anger. Carlson didn't fit the profile. Have you asked Andrew's old mistress if he hit her?"

"No, Julie and I didn't ask her about his violent tendencies, but I think a repeat visit is warranted. I also want to visit the museum where that sword is hanging."

"Why?"

"Because I want to talk to the curator, ask about the effort it takes to hack apart a body like what was done to Catherine." He stood.

"You could ask the coroner."

"But a historian might be able to give me a better picture. He would be more familiar with the use of swords."

"You're right. I never thought of it in that way."

The smile she gave him nearly melted him. If Kelly didn't want to continue what they had started out on the porch, then he had better beat a hasty exit. "I need to get going."

"Sure." She seemed startled at his abruptness.

He folded the sheet he'd made notes on and tucked it into the pocket of his sport coat.

"Jake reminded me earlier about the next fund-raiser

that we're scheduled to attend.'' She fiddled with papers on the desk. ''It's tomorrow night. A barbecue.''

''I assume you want me to dress accordingly.''

''At least you don't have to wear a tux.''

''Just boots and a hat.'' As he walked down the hall, he glanced at the closed door. He wanted to ask Kelly if she ever went into that room but kept his mouth shut.

He paused at the front door. ''What time tomorrow night?''

''Six-thirty.''

Get out before you do something stupid, his mind yelled. ''I'll see you then.'' He walked to his car without looking back.

As he drove off, he waved at Mrs. Schattle.

''If you turn at the next street, the Coffee Cup should be on the corner,'' Julie instructed Ash.

Ash eyed his partner. The store was located at the end of the long block where Reed's home stood.

''I've stopped a couple of times to get a cup of coffee. It makes the late night interesting.''

''So, I should let you take over the questioning?'' Ash asked.

''I'm not that familiar with anyone. But they might respond to me since I've been in there before and I'm a little less intimidating.''

''My ass,'' Ash grumbled. He pulled up into the parking lot of the trendy little coffee shop. The rich aroma of roasting coffee beans filled the place.

''May I help you?'' the teenage girl asked around her gum.

''I need to talk to your manager,'' Julie told the girl. When she hesitated, Julie added, ''We're the police and need to talk to him.''

The girl disappeared into the back room. Moments later a man in the late thirties walked up. "What can I do for you?"

After the introductions were made, Julie asked, "Is there someone here who would've worked here five years ago?"

"No. I started managing this location four years ago."

"None of your employees were here then?" Julie followed up.

"I'm lucky if I can keep my employees five months, let alone five years."

"Is there anyone we might talk to who could tell us about this store that long ago?" Ash questioned.

"Exactly what dates are you looking at?"

"July 20," Ash replied.

The man held up his finger. "Wait a minute. Let me go and check something." He disappeared into the back room. Within five minutes he reappeared, a log in his hands. "On that date, this store was closed. There was an electrical fire and it was shut down for three days, the seventeenth through the twentieth."

Ash and Julie smiled at each other.

"Thank you," Julie said. "You've been a big help."

"No problem."

The main door opened and Andrew Reed waltzed in. He stopped when he spotted Ash.

"Detective Ashcroft, what are you doing here?"

"Just checking out a lead," Ash casually replied.

"On what?" Andrew asked.

Ash smiled pleasantly. "Yours was not the only case that HPD was working on."

The manager looked from Ash to Andrew. He disappeared into the back room.

Andrew Reed stiffened. "Of course." He walked to the counter to order.

When they were in the car, Ash shook his head. "So our lead suspect doesn't have an alibi. Why do you suppose Ralph didn't check it out?"

"Why don't you ask Detective Lee?" Julie replied.

Ash put the car in gear. "I think I'll do just that."

Ash walked into Captain Jenkins's office and closed the door. Jenkins raised his brow.

"We've got a problem. Andrew Reed's alibi is fiction and Detective Lee didn't check it out."

Jenkins's expression hardened. "How do you know?"

"Julie and I looked into it today. That store was closed due to fire damage the day Catherine died. I thought about confronting Lee about why he didn't check it out, but I decided to run it by you first.

"Also, we've learned the fiancée's family is loaded. Reed has managed to go through Catherine's estate at an alarming rate. Several deals have gone south on him. I haven't talked to the parties involved, but I will."

Jenkins tapped his fingers on the desktop. "Why don't you wait on talking to Lee. Let's see what else you come up with."

Ash nodded and reached for the door. He paused, his hand on the knob. He looked back to his boss.

"What's wrong, Ash?"

"When we started this investigation, I told Kelly that Ralph Lee had the best closure rate in the department. She gave me a skeptical look and wondered if the rest of his cases were as shoddy as this one." He rubbed the back of his neck. "It's made me wonder, Captain.

And now, after discovering this, about the Reed alibi, her comments are eating me alive.''

"You've got a point. Keep working on this case. I'll look into it.''

Ash knew that Captain Jenkins was a careful, honest cop. If he said he would check, he would.

"All right.'' Ash pulled open the door.

"Ash.''

He paused.

"Have a good time tonight.'' Captain Jenkins grinned.

"That's what I want, to mix with the polite folks playing cowboy. But I'm not riding any mechanical bulls.''

Jenkins's laughter followed Ash.

Ash knocked on Kelly's door at six-thirty. His gut warned him to be on guard. He glanced around the neighborhood to see if anyone was watching. He didn't doubt Mrs. Schattle was, but she wouldn't produce this feeling.

Kelly opened the door. Her hair was tumbling out of its twist and her blouse was pulled out of her skirt, the top button undone. He could see the dark shadow between her breasts.

"I'm sorry I'm running late.'' She swept her appearance with her hand. "I got caught in court, then Craig decided he wanted to be chatty.'' She stepped back and motioned him inside. "Apparently, our reunion is the talk of the D.A.'s office.'' She shook her head. "Everyone wants to give advice or get hot information. I nearly laughed in Craig's face when he was telling me how to handle a romance with my ex. I wanted to ask him how well he did with his.''

"If it's any comfort to you, the other detectives are looking at me as if I've lost all my sense. Their consensus is that I'm nuts."

"Oh, that's real flattering to me."

His gaze flew to her face. Mischief sparkled in her eyes.

"Go get dressed, Counselor."

Grinning, she walked into her bedroom but didn't close the door. "Give me five minutes to change."

Well, Ash could now identify the warning he'd felt, and it had nothing to do with the bad guys. It was this thing building between Kelly and himself.

Damn.

"It was a miserable day at work. I had two new cases just assigned. Trying to schedule depositions, talking to defense attorneys. You should've seen the scam one of the lawyers tried on us." Her voice drifted in and out. He stepped closer to hear.

"What was it?"

She laughed and it did amazing things to him. "He quickly changed his tune after he talked to me, and I told him the unimpeachable witnesses we had. Also videotape from the store. I don't doubt he'll want to cut a deal."

Ash was reminded what an excellent attorney his ex was and what enthusiasm she brought to her work. And how she didn't cut corners. He'd forgotten her strengths in the turmoil of their divorce.

"I have good news on the Carlson case."

She appeared at the bedroom door. Jeans hugged her legs and the blue western shirt hung out from the denim. Her feet were bare. "What?"

"Andrew's alibi is complete fiction."

She stepped closer. "How?"

"Julie and I went to the coffee bar that Andrew claims to have gone for a drink. The place was closed due to a fire."

"Why didn't Detective Lee discover this?"

"I don't know. I talked to my boss about asking Lee, but we're going to wait. We did run into Andrew at the coffee bar. He asked why we were there."

"And what was your answer?"

"Police business. He looked like he wanted to bust a gut."

"Good. Let him twist in the wind." She held up her hand. "I'm almost ready. Five minutes." She disappeared into the bedroom.

He wandered around the living room. Plants were placed around the room. That was another of Kelly's passions—gardening.

He glanced down at the Oriental carpet covering the floor. He remembered when they had found this treasure at an estate sale. Kelly had been giddy with delight to find it. She was still in school and he in patrol. Neither had money, but when they saw this carpet, they paid the outrageous price.

"I'm ready."

He turned to view her. She'd pulled her hair into a ponytail at the base of her neck. Her western belt and cowboy boots gave her an authentic look. He remembered when she had bought those boots. They'd gone to get him a pair of boots, then the salesman had talked her into some, as well.

"Let's go and see what information we can collect tonight at the Sweeney's barbecue."

Emory Sweeney smiled at Kelly.

"It's so good to see you, young lady. I'm glad you came to this dog-and-pony show."

Kelly laughed and glanced around the flagstone patio. Trees shaded the area and a large garden was blooming with various colors of azaleas. Decorative pots scattered around the area were filled with blooms. "You're the one who's throwing this event."

He grinned. "I have to keep up my influence in this city. It's a small price to pay." He nodded to Ash. "It's good to see you." He extended his hand.

Ash grasped the old man's hand.

"Tell me. I've heard that you two are causing talk. You decided, since Hawk got married, to take the plunge yourself?"

Kelly's heart nearly stopped. She turned to Ash, wondering at his reaction.

He slipped his arm around Kelly. "While working on the Carlson retrial, we discovered we still have things in common."

Emory looked from Ash to Kelly. She wanted to squirm under his careful examination. He stepped closer. "I'll warn you that the Procters are supposed to be here tonight."

Terrific. "Thanks for the warning." She nodded, then wrapped her arm around Ash's and started forward. "I'm glad he warned us," she whispered.

"Don't worry. I doubt they'll want to speak to either of us," he answered.

It proved to be one of the few times Kelly could remember that Ash was flat-out wrong. The instant the Procters spotted them, they bore down on Ash and Kelly like a hawk on a mouse.

"What is going on, young woman, that your detective there is asking our family lawyer questions about Catherine?'' Mr. Procter demanded, pointing at Ash.

''We thought this mess was finished,'' Mrs. Procter added.

The elderly couple glared at them and Kelly felt Ash's body tighten.

''We were trying to tie up loose ends,'' Kelly offered, hoping that her innocuous comment would satisfy them.

''Such as?'' Mr. Procter demanded.

Kelly debated for a moment about the wisdom of her move, but instinct told her to go for it. ''Did you know that your daughter had seen your family attorney about obtaining a divorce?''

Both Mr. and Mrs. Procter stared at her as if she'd grown a second head.

''That's not true,'' Mrs. Procter protested.

''It is according to a friend of your daughter's and your family lawyer.''

Mr. Procter glared at them. ''That is a lie. Divorce has never disgraced our family.''

That explained a lot about why Catherine had dropped the proceedings.

''If these slanderous rumors aren't stopped, I'll make sure the D.A. doesn't win this next election,'' Mr. Procter continued.

''Is that a threat?'' Ash quietly asked, the deadly menace clear.

Clearly the old man wasn't used to people challenging him. ''It's a warning.'' He grabbed his wife and marched off.

Kelly sagged against Ash. ''I guess I blew that. But I now know Catherine didn't tell her parents that she and Andrew were having trouble.''

''Or maybe, she told them, but they ignored her and

that's why they are so upset about what's happening now.''

What Ash said made sense. The Procters exhibited all the classic signs of guilt. ''It might help us if we could discover if Catherine had confided in her parents.''

''I'll add it to the list of things that need to be checked out.'' He scanned the crowd. ''We might want to give Jake a heads-up that these folks are gunning for him.''

Kelly closed her eyes. She didn't want to do that, but Jake deserved a warning. ''Let's find him.''

Ash watched as Kelly talked to her boss. From this distance, it appeared that Jake wasn't happy.

''You look like you've lost your best friend,'' Hawk commented, stopping by Ash's side.

''Naw. I'm just watching as Kelly explains the little faux pas that occurred earlier.''

Hawk raised his brow. ''What was that?''

''We had a little run-in with the Procters. Apparently their daughter checked into getting a divorce from her husband. Either her parents didn't know or didn't want to know.'' He shrugged. ''We were given the line that Procters don't divorce.''

Hawk shook his head. ''They're from the old school that don't do divorce.''

Ash frowned.

''There are still those folks who haven't come into the current age. I bet if they own a computer, they hire someone to run it for them.''

The idea caught. ''That's a good point. If they have a personal secretary, that individual might know if Catherine told her parents about wanting a divorce.''

"Why are you still checking into that? I thought you suspended that investigation." Hawk studied Ash, then his eyes widened. "You didn't drop the case, did you?"

Ash nodded toward the edge of the patio away from other people. When they were alone, he said, "You guessed it."

"Captain Jenkins okay with that?"

"We've got it covered. Both Jenkins and Thorpe are in. But because of the howling from certain quarters, we've decided to tackle it in a less—publ—"

"I get it. So the dating your ex-wife is part of this cover?" Hawk's gaze searched his.

"Yup."

Doubt laced his gaze. "And that's all?" he pressed.

Ash knew exactly what Hawk was asking. But he wasn't ready to admit anything but his job. "That's all."

"Sure."

From Hawk's tone, Ash knew he hadn't fooled his ex-partner.

Kelly nodded to her boss and walked toward them.

"How did it go?" Ash questioned.

Kelly glanced at Hawk.

"He knows," Ash informed her.

She shrugged. "Jake wasn't thrilled, but he didn't back down. He told me to continue. If he lost his job, he lost it, but justice was to be pursued." She smiled. "I knew there was a reason I admired him."

"Then we're still going forward."

"We are."

Hawk studied them. "Do you need any help this afternoon?"

"Just keep your ears open, see if you hear anything about Catherine or Andrew and his new love. We also want to know if Andrew was abusive to his wife or his ex-mistress,'' Ash answered.

"I haven't ever heard about him beating Catherine, but it was common knowledge that you didn't want to anger him. Why don't we talk to my father-in-law, Emory Sweeney. He might be able to shed some light on the subject."

A baby's gurgle floated through the air. Hawk's head came up and turned. His face completely changed from no-nonsense lawyer to a man enthralled when he saw his wife and young daughter. It always amazed Ash the change in Hawk when Renee came into his life. With the birth of their daughter, Hawk had become a puddle of emotion. Who would have thought such a thing could happen? Hawk's face bore a very different expression from any Ash had witnessed in the years he'd partnered with him.

"I saw you two with your heads together over here. What are you planning?" Renee asked, stepping to Hawk's side.

"Nothing," Hawk answered, pulling the baby from Renee's hold and settling her in the crook of his arm.

"Don't try to play me, Matthew Hawkins." The teasing expression in Renee's eyes softened her words.

"We're talking about Andrew Reed and that big society murder several years ago," Ash volunteered.

"What about that case?"

"Have you heard about anything about his temper?" Ash pressed.

"No, but the man reminds me of Hawk's ex-wife— sleazy and not someone I wanted to know or trust."

Kelly's eyes widened at the reference, but Hawk simply laughed. "Yeah, now that I think about it, they do seem to have a lot in common. Interested in money."

Renee shared a look with Hawk. "But probably the best person to talk to is Dad. He knows a great deal about the elite of society." She turned and scanned the crowd for her father. "Give me a minute to find him."

Hawk looked at the child in his arms. "Isn't she the most beautiful baby you've ever seen?"

Kelly's eyes softened and her fingers brushed the baby's cheek. "Yes, she's beautiful. Mind if I hold her?"

Hawk gave Kelly his daughter. Kelly's face softened as she gazed into the baby's blue eyes. As she softly rocked the little girl, Ash noticed the moisture in her eyes. She quickly wiped her eye and smiled at the child. Suddenly the picture of Kelly holding a baby—their daughter—flashed into his mind, bringing pain and regret.

"Kelly, Ash, Dad's waiting for us in the library." Renee stepped to Kelly's side and took the squirming bundle. "Mind if I come and listen?"

"Not at all," Kelly answered.

The library was Ash's favorite room in this massive house. Walls of books, floor to ceiling. The large freestanding globe and massive desk proclaimed that this man had money.

Emory sat in a dark leather chair by the fireplace. He motioned Kelly and Ash to the sofa across from him. Renee and Hawk settled on the opposite sofa.

"I hear you want to pump me for information about Andrew Reed." Emory smiled. "So pump."

"I wouldn't exactly label it that way," Kelly began.

"But that's what it amounts to, isn't it? You remember, young woman, I've been doing this kind of thing in the city of Houston since before you were born."

The crusty old man had a point. "Yes, but this information could be very vital to our investigation,'' she answered.

His eyes narrowed. "So the D.A. didn't drop the case of the Reed murder?"

"No," Ash replied, wanting to spare Kelly the brunt of the responsibility. "But it's easier to proceed under the table without the grief we get from certain people."

Emory nodded. "I understand and sympathize. So tell me, what is it you want to know?"

"Have you heard rumors about Andrew Reed having a nasty temper?" Kelly asked.

He thought a moment. "No, I can't say that I have. But I'll tell you that if you can't benefit Andrew, he doesn't want anything to do with you. The man's only love is himself. Soon after Catherine married him, I invited him to a charity event, a golf tournament, I sponsored for deprived youths. He golfed the first time, but from his attitude, I knew that the only reason he did it was to keep his in-laws happy. When I asked him again, he politely refused, making the excuse of a previous engagement. But I knew that it would be a cold day in hell before he'd give any more of his time or money. I didn't ask again."

"So you never heard of him hitting his wife?" Ash asked.

"No, I can't say I have. But I will tell you that I once heard a couple of the servants at a party saying that he nearly chewed off the servant's head for spilling a drink on him."

Kelly sighed. "Unfortunately, that describes any number of people in his social set."

"Edna May Vanderslice," Renee blurted out. The baby fussed and Renee brushed her fingers over the child's cheek. She sighed and went back to sleep.

"Who?" Kelly questioned.

"Surely you know her." Renee's eyes widened. "My husband still shivers at the mention of that old lady."

Hawk laughed. "I do, indeed, but there's an honest woman, who sees through the act of most people." He turned to his wife. "Isn't she here?"

"I don't—"

"She is," Emory interrupted. "Why don't we go find her and you can question her yourself."

Renee and Kelly found Edna May signing a check in her support of Jake. The tiny old woman, with steel-gray hair and piercing brown eyes, smiled with she saw the baby.

"Ah, let me see that darling girl," Edna May said. After she patted the baby's head, she winked at Renee. "I told you that you got a good one and this little one just proves it."

Renee flushed. "You did, indeed. Edna May, this is Kelly Whalen of the D.A.'s office. She wants to ask you a couple of questions."

The old woman carefully studied Kelly. "Ah, you're here with that good-looking cop. I'd grab him up, but it looks like you did."

Kelly's heart jerked.

"What is it you want to know?" Edna May asked.

Gathering her thoughts, Kelly asked, "I want know what you know about Andrew Reed."

"That he's a SOB. Anything else?"

Renee laughed. "I told you that she'd tell it like it is."

Kelly cleared her throat. "There are still questions that haven't been answered about Catherine Reed's murder."

"It's about time someone was asking them." Her eyes hardened. "I was there that night when that little lady walked in and saw that jerk with his mistress, her pinned up against the wall and him—" She took a deep breath. "I would've shot the bastard then and there and not let him shame me that way. But Catherine was too much a lady, thought too much about what her parents would say if she pitched a fit. She should have." Edna shook her head. "I don't doubt Catherine and Andrew had words on the way home. The way she was murdered was vicious.

"I'll say this for Catherine—she didn't have a bad temper. But she did have a great deal of pride. To have been shamed that way wouldn't have gone down easily." She studied Kelly. "That help?"

Kelly grinned. "Yes, it does."

Edna May nodded. "Good. You get him."

Kelly prayed she could do exactly that.

Edna turned back to Kelly. "And you need to get that good-looking detective, too."

Chapter 11

Ash leaned against the outside brick of the mansion and watched as Kelly and Renee talked to Edna May Vanderslice. Edna—shriveled up prune of a woman—said something and the surprised expression on Kelly's face made him smile.

"That's quite a lady," Jacob Blackhorse commented.

Ash turned and studied his old friend. They'd worked together with Hawk when Renee's life had been threatened. Ash liked the quiet man, who was the head of security for Texas Chic, Emory's company.

"Who are you talking about?" Ash asked.

Jacob frowned. "Edna May. Who'd you think I was talking about?" He glanced back at the group and a dawning light entered his eyes. He turned to Ash. "You thought I meant Kelly? So it's true. You're dating your ex-wife?" A slow smile creased his mouth. "Well, it certainly has caused talk at this party."

Great, he and Kelly were the hottest item of gossip among the moneyed.

"What's going on, friend?" Jacob asked.

"So everyone believes that Kelly and I are an item?"

Jacob studied Ash. "It rivals the talk about Catherine Reed's murder and the death of her murderer." He took a sip of his beer. "And I know that earlier confrontation between Kelly and the Procters is on everyone's mind."

"I don't know whether to be glad that our cover is working or not." Ash ran his fingers through his hair.

"So you're not seeing each other again?"

Ash wanted to squirm under Jacob's intense scrutiny. "We're running an investigation. What do you know about Andrew Reed?"

Jacob hesitated a moment, then said, "Not much. He likes money and shows it off. And I don't like him."

The little meeting across the patio between the ladies broke up. Kelly saw them and walked to Ash's side. She greeted Jacob.

"Did you discover anything interesting?" Ash asked.

She glanced at Jacob.

"I told him," Ash explained.

"Miss Edna was just another confirmation that Andrew Reed is a miserable human being."

Jacob laughed. "I agree with that assessment."

Kelly turned to him. "Really?"

He shrugged. "It's part of the job to endure unpleasant rich folks like Andrew."

She nodded, but Ash saw something else in her eyes that she'd learned.

"What else did Edna May say?" Ash asked.

Her gaze slid away from his. "Nothing."

He decided not to push her now. When he took her home, he'd discover what she had learned.

"Ash," Julie McKinney called out to him. His partner, dressed in black slacks and a white shirt, emerged from the crowd. She nodded to Jacob. "Joanna Kris was shot. It appears it was a home robbery. Ralph Lee took the case."

"Where is she?"

"She's been taken to Ben Taub."

"Did they catch the shooter?"

"Not so far," Julie replied.

Ash looked at Kelly.

"You go," Kelly encouraged. "I'll get myself home."

He handed her his keys. "Take my car. I'll have Julie drop me by your place afterward."

As he left the party, he glanced back at Kelly. She and Jacob made a fine-looking couple. It was a disturbing thought.

But oddly enough, Jacob's gaze wasn't fixed on Kelly, but on Julie.

"I guess you've ended more than one party this way, with Ash being called away," Jacob commented.

Kelly turned to him and forced a smile. "It's happened more than once." She remembered other times, more intimate times when Ash had been called away.

"Mind if I ask why you're so interested in Joanna?" Jacob probed.

"It's part of the investigation Ash and I are on now."

Jacob's brown eyes twinkled. "So I can't pump you for information." Admiration filled his gaze. He was a handsome man with black hair, teak skin and a killer smile. Too bad that package didn't resonate in her. But, if she didn't miss her guess, it did with Julie McKinney. That would be an interesting match.

"You didn't expect me to give away anything," she shot back.

He shrugged. "It was entertaining watching you with Edna May."

Kelly laughed. "I hadn't ever met the lady, but I must say it was an experience."

"Well, I've seen her eat many a debutante for hors d'oeuvres."

Kelly's stomach grumbled, stopping Jacob.

"May I get you a plate of barbecue?"

"That's the best offer I've had all night."

He shook his head. "I seriously doubt that."

Ash and Julie passed Ralph Lee in the lobby of the hospital. He frowned at them. "What are you doing here?"

"How's Joanna Kris?" Ash replied.

His eyes narrowed. "She's in surgery. They're going to call when she's out and can be interviewed. But you didn't answer my question."

"We think whoever shot Joanna might be the same guy who's been doing a lot of home invasions in that neighborhood where one of the victims was killed," Julie offered. "We wanted to check it out."

Ralph's face relaxed. "I'll let you know when you can talk to the victim."

"Thanks, Ralph." Julie turned to Ash. "C'mon, partner, let's go."

Ash didn't argue with her, knowing she was on a mission. Once they were in the car, she said, "Why don't we go and look at the crime scene?"

"My thoughts exactly."

It took only fifteen minutes to get to Joanna's house.

The last crime-scene detective was finishing up, and no one questioned Ash and Julie's presence.

"Hey, Dave, how's it going?" Ash glanced around the living room. A spot of blood marred the white carpet by the sofa.

"Can't complain. You doing this case? I thought it was Ralph's."

"We interviewed the victim last week and wondered if it had any connection with that case. We wanted to look around. What did you find?"

Dave closed his evidence case. "There's no sign of forced entry. Nothing out of place. It looks like the shooter walked in and shot the victim who, unless I miss my guess, was sitting on the couch, because of the blood on the cushion. She probably stood, was shot again and fell, since there was blood on the carpet."

Ash and Julie surveyed the room.

"Any more questions?"

Ash studied his partner and she shook her head. "Not now," Ash replied.

"Throw the lock when you're finished."

Julie nodded. When they were alone, they walked slowly through the house, then walked a grid of the living room.

"I've got the feeling this is connected to Catherine's murder," Julie said.

Ash moved to the piano. "Wasn't there a picture here when we were here the last time?" A vase of flowers stood where the picture had been.

"Yeah, there was."

"Andrew and Joanna in a happier time. Why don't we look for it?" he said.

After twenty minutes, they found the picture buried

under a stack of towels in the hall linen closet next to the bathroom.

Ash stared at the picture of Joanna and Andrew, the mayor and the quarterback of the Rice Owls smiling for the camera, drinks in their hands, formal evening clothes.

"From where we found this, it looks like Joanna is mad at her old boyfriend," Julie commented, handing Ash the frame, "but I don't see anything off-kilter in this picture."

He couldn't see anything, either. "Or maybe she didn't want us to see the picture of her and her boyfriend if we came back." He studied the people surrounding the smiling couple.

"What are you looking at?" Julie asked.

"I was wondering when that picture was taken and at what party."

"Maybe we should ask Joanna when we can talk to her."

"I think you're right." He put back the photo. "You want to drive me to Kelly's so I can pick up my car?"

Julie gave him a speculative look. "Yeah."

"What's that look for?" he demanded.

"Nothing, Ash. Nothing."

It didn't sound like nothing.

As Kelly pulled out of the driveway of the mansion in Ash's Jeep, she took a deep breath. It had been a rough night. Confronting the Procters, then fighting off all the speculative glances from friends and society folks. Apparently she and Ash didn't have trouble making people believe their cover story of reunited lovers.

It felt so right to be in his arms, having him beside her as she moved through a crowd. His presence behind her when she tangled with the Procters had given her strength and comfort. She knew she wasn't alone in the battle. She also knew she could depend on him, on his observations.

Pulling into the driveway of her house, the memory of finding this place washed over her. They'd just married and needed to move from the cramped efficiency where she'd lived. Ash had fallen over several of her law books and sprained his ankle. The next day, they'd gone looking for another place.

"Stop it, Kelly," she muttered. "You don't need a walk down memory lane."

Opening the front door, Kelly tried to concentrate on what information they'd gathered tonight. She went to her office and quickly input the information that Edna May had given her. The old woman's encouragement to go after Ash also reverberated through her.

Kelly printed out her notes and reread them. Had she missed anything?

An image of Renee holding her baby girl popped into her head. She was a beautiful child, the obvious joy of both her parents. Kelly stood and moved down the hall to the closed door. She opened it and turned on the light. The cheerful nursery looked eerie. And sad.

An emptiness washed over her.

Slowly Kelly walked into the room. She stopped by the crib and picked up the large teddy bear. Tears made the bear waver. She stumbled over to the rocker and sank into it. Holding the bear to her chest, tears began to flow.

She didn't know how long she had sat there. She thought she heard her name, then suddenly Ash knelt before her. His hand cupped her chin. When her eyes met his, she saw the sadness there. He stood and pulled her into his arms.

His warmth surrounded her, comforting her, pulling her out of the darkness. She felt his hands rubbing lightly over her back. His lips touched her temple.

"She would've been four. Like Sarah," she whispered.

"I know." Ash cupped her head and drew it to his chest. "I know."

Her arms wrapped around him as they shared the quiet grief they both felt. She didn't know how long she held him. Time had no meaning. But when the knot of emotion had eased, she felt a sense of peace.

His hands stilled. She glanced up and saw tears hanging off his chin. Her fingers trembled as she wiped away the moisture. His lips turned into a sad smile. Slowly he lowered his head and gently kissed her.

Suddenly the air between them changed, became charged with the energy of their body heat. Longing and attraction enveloped them. Her heart thundered and the need to taste his lips again raced through her.

She welcomed his mouth, meeting his eagerness with her own. His tongue slipped into her mouth, tasting, coaxing hers into a dance. Her hands clenched the back of his shirt, holding on for dear life.

He kissed his way across her chin and found the sensitive area under her chin. Her head fell back to give him access.

When she heard the thundering, she thought it was her heart, but Ash stopped and looked up. Her eyes opened and she frowned.

"What?"

"Someone's at the front door."

Kelly came out of her fog and walked from the nursery. She felt Ash behind her. When she opened the front door, Julie stood there.

"We need to go downtown. They caught the guy who matches Sarah Mendoza's description of the killer of Steve Carlson."

"How did they catch him?" Ash asked.

"He had an altercation with his neighbor. Took out his gun and shot him."

"Where are my keys?" Ash asked Kelly.

"They're on my desk, but I want to go, too," Kelly said. "I want to be there when you interview him."

"Fine, but I need my keys."

She retrieved them. "I'll follow you in case you get caught at headquarters."

As she followed Ash, Kelly was grateful for the interruption. At the rate they'd been going, they would have been on the floor, tearing each other's clothes off. Her sanity had fled, leaving her without a clear thought. What had she been thinking?

The lights in the jail were jarring, dispelling any of the soft feelings she'd shared with Ash. Sarah's description of the suspect, Bruce Rhodes, was right on the mark. Kelly observed as Ash and Kelly questioned the man about the murder of Steve Carlson. He said nothing, only demanded his lawyer.

Kelly met the detectives in the lobby of the jail.

"This old boy been around the track a few times. He knows the drill. We'll show his booking shot to the people in the apartment complex where Carlson lived."

"You might check to see if the suspect served any time with Carlson," Kelly suggested.

"Good idea." Ash walked Kelly to her car. "Anything else happen after I left the party?"

"Nope. But I did learn our cover is working. Prob-

ably too well. That's all anyone wanted to talk about,''
she grumbled.

He laughed.

''What's so funny?''

''I'm being hit with the same reaction and the same
questions. It makes me wonder—'' When he looked
into her eyes, that electricity was still there, throbbing,
pulsing.

Kelly wanted to talk to him about their baby, her
feelings, her pain. It was an odd feeling. ''Ash, thank
you.''

''For what?''

''For tonight.'' She didn't say anything more, but
from the look in his eyes, she knew he understood her
meaning.

He nodded. ''Good night, Kel.'' He walked to his
car.

She wanted to call him back, ask him to come back
home with her, but in the cold light of reality, she knew
she wasn't ready for that step. She wished things could
have been different. But some things, she knew,
couldn't be fixed.

Ash stared at the red light. What had just happened
between Kelly and him? When he'd walked into the
house earlier tonight, he'd known something was
wrong. The door was unlocked.

A horn behind him jerked him from the memories.
Hawk and Renee's baby reminded both Kelly and him
of what they'd lost. He'd been able to avoid those feelings for years, but seeing the bear in Kelly's arms and
the tears in her eyes, he couldn't stop the surge of grief.

Together they had cried and ached.

He pulled into the parking lot of his apartment complex and found an empty space close to his unit. Once inside the darkened apartment, he didn't turn on the light. Throwing himself on the couch, he rested his head.

He needed to think, strip away the emotions. Tomorrow he and Julie needed to take the picture of the suspect to the apartment where Carlson lived—

The sight of Kelly with the bear in her arms popped into his head. He pushed it aside.

They needed to talk to the Procters' servants, too, to see if they knew about Catherine filing for divorce. It wouldn't be bad idea to interview the servants at the Reed home, also—

Kelly's pain had mingled with his. It was the first time he had let tears flow.

Think about the case.

There was also that picture. It bothered Ash. When and if Joanna Kris woke up, he intended to question her about it—

If Julie hadn't shown up, he would have taken Kelly to their bedroom and pulled her onto the bed and made love to her.

He threw his arm over his eyes. He was in trouble.

Kelly picked up the white teddy bear from the floor and put it back into the crib. She should feel embarrassed by her breakdown, but she didn't. She felt lighter. The only other person who knew what she was feeling was Ash.

When she saw the tears on his face, it had touched a deep hurt inside her that was tender. He'd hurt, too. She'd always thought she'd been alone in her grief, but now she knew differently.

The emptiness was still there, but it had changed

somehow, softening, easing. She finger-combed the hair on the bear's face and placed him back in the corner of the crib.

With a final look around the room, she turned off the light but didn't close the door.

If Julie hadn't come, would she have let Ash make love to her? Did she want that?

Those were questions that she didn't want to answer.

Joanna Kris regained consciousness the next morning. She looked tired and defeated hooked up to all the equipment in the ICU. She eyed Ash and Julie.

"Did you recognize who shot you?" Ash asked.

She looked away from them. "No."

Julie stepped closer. "Why did you let him in?"

"He said he had flowers for me." She turned to look at Ash. "What woman doesn't want flowers?"

"Did he attempt to rob you?" Ash questioned.

"No."

"Did he say why he wanted to hurt you?" Ash pressed.

"No."

Obviously the attempted murder had had its desired effect—it had shut Joanna up.

Julie pulled the photo of the suspect, Bruce Rhodes, they'd nabbed last night. They'd found a set of overalls from a florist shop in his apartment. She showed the mug shot to Joanna. "Is this the man who shot you?"

Joanna went pale and turned away. "No."

Ash knew a lie when he heard it.

"What happened to the picture of you and Andrew that was on your piano, Joanna?" he asked.

"I didn't want to see it anymore. I put it away."

Julie touched Joanna's arm. "When was it taken?"

"Several years ago at a party."

"Which one?"

Joanna closed her eyes and turned her head away. "I don't know. I'm tired. Please go."

As they walked out of the hospital, Julie said, "I think Joanna was lying through her teeth."

"She was."

They drove to the apartment building where Carlson lived and showed the picture to Sarah.

"Is that the man, sweetie?" Julie asked.

Her solemn eyes regarded the detectives. "Yes." She clutched her mother's leg and pressed her face into the fabric of her mother's jeans.

The woman glared at the detectives. "You've frightened her. Go away."

Ash opened his mouth to argue, but Julie's hand on his arm stopped him.

Maria nodded. "You will not be here when she wakes in the middle of the night crying. I will not do this to her again." With those final words, she closed the apartment door in their faces.

Julie glanced at her partner. "I can't blame the mother. Sarah's given us more than most of the folks we've interviewed."

He agreed, but Sarah was the best bet they had.

When they went to the jail to further question Bruce Rhodes, they discovered that he'd made bail.

"Damn. Who would've thought the system worked that fast?" Ash ran his fingers through his hair and cursed. Worry ate at him. "I wonder who sprang our suspect?"

"I've been looking for you, Ash," the watch commander said as he walked out of his office.

"Why?" Ash asked.

"Your ex-wife's house was broken into. A Mrs. Schattle called the 911 operator and reported it. She said to notify you and Kelly."

Where was Kelly? Was she at home or had she been at work? "You heard back from the unit on scene?" Ash questioned.

"Not yet."

"Thanks. I'll call Kelly."

Ash went to his desk and called the D.A.'s office, discovering that Kelly was in court. He didn't like the feel of the situation. "I'm going over to the court building to tell Kelly what's happened."

The trip across downtown took less than five minutes. Running inside, he went to the courtroom where Kelly should have been. The room was empty. He tracked down the court supervisor and learned the judge had been sick and postponed the trial.

"Do you know where the A.D.A. is?" he asked the woman.

"No."

A coldness settled around his heart.

"Mary, do you know what happened to Kelly Whalen?" the woman asked the girl at the next desk.

"When she was in rescheduling, she mentioned something about working out some of the tension in her neck."

Ash stared at the women. "Do you know what she was talking about?"

The older woman smiled. "I do. There's a massage place in front of evidence storage."

Ash knew the place. "Thanks."

Ash didn't see Kelly's car but decided to check out the place anyway.

He flashed his badge to the receptionist. "Is A.D.A. Kelly Whalen here?"

The woman studied him. "Yes."

Relief rushed through him, followed by blood-boiling anger. "What room is she in?"

"Room four. But you can't—"

He shoved his badge into his pocket and marched down the hall.

Kelly sighed, enjoying the skilled hands working out the knots in her neck. This morning after her first post-ponement, she had decided she deserved an hour's break and a full massage. Between Ash, the Procters and the sterling Andrew Reed, it had been a miserable week. She had discovered this place when one of the other A.D.A.'s who had vicious tension headaches talked about it.

The soft sound of the ocean played in the background while the female therapist worked the knots out of her shoulders.

"You're very tense," her therapist murmured.

She didn't know the half of it. Kelly let her mind drift and the image that popped into her mind was of Ash, his fingers on her, his skin touching hers.

"Where is she?" Kelly heard Ash demand, his voice harsh. He sounded as if he wanted to scare the recep-tionist spitless.

So much for relaxation.

"Room four," came the reply. "But you can't—"

Before Kelly could react, the door to the small room opened and Ash barreled inside. Kelly glanced over her shoulder.

Ash stopped and stared at her bare back. "What the hell are you doing?" He had a wild-eyed look to him.

"Getting a massage." Kelly turned over, but the sheet covering her bare torso slipped. She felt Ash's stare burning into her, making her breasts peak. Grabbing the sheet, she yanked it up over her breasts. The heat in his brown eyes nearly incinerated the table.

"You can't barge in here," the therapist protested.

Ash flashed his badge. When the woman started to protest, Kelly shook her head.

"It's okay."

The therapist left.

"What's wrong?" Kelly asked, sliding off the table.

His eyes continued to stare at her chest. She felt the pull of the attraction sucking her down into a vortex.

He shook his head. "Mrs. Schattle called the cops."

"So? She calls on a regular basis."

"This time your house was broken into. The watch commander came looking for me when Mrs. Schattle told the operator to contact you and me. And Bruce Rhodes made bail."

"What?" His urgency was understandable. "Who let that slip through?" After several seconds when he hadn't moved but stood rooted to the spot, she said, "If you'll step outside, Ash, I'll get dressed and we can see about my house."

"Sure."

Kelly quickly dressed, gathered her purse and walked to the back door.

"I'll follow you," Ash informed her.

Kelly closed her eyes. They had trouble.

The patrol car was still at the house, as well as crime scene and a detective from burglary.

Ash felt like a fool for blowing up at Kelly the way he had, but when he saw her, saw all that beautiful smooth skin, his worry for her safety had ambushed him.

He walked with Kelly through the house. The detective, Eric Montgomery, glanced up and nodded to Ash and Kelly. The library was a mess. Files were dumped onto the floor where they had been pulled from the filing cabinet. Her desk was a disaster with papers littering the surface.

"I'll need you to see if there's anything missing, Kelly, here and in the rest of the house," Eric said.

She glanced at Ash. He knew exactly what she suspected. It was the same suspicion he had.

"I'll check. Why don't I walk through the house, then we can go through the files in this room when your guys are finished."

"Sounds good," Eric agreed.

As she walked into the living, she said, "It's odd that I decided to take the Carlson file with me this morning. It's in my briefcase."

His eyes widened. "Why'd you do that?"

"I had one of those funny feelings that I should take that file with me today. Looks like you're not the only one with good instincts."

"You're right."

Kelly slowly walked through each room of the house. Ash followed. The crime-scene guys had dusted the window in the living room where the intruder had pried it open and slipped inside.

"Did you lift any prints off the window, Eric?" Ash called.

"Not any reliable ones," he yelled back.

Ash glanced at the broken lock. "I'll fix it. We'll go to the hardware store and buy another lock. Of course, it's a lousy lock, and I won't be surprised if it was just a teenager, looking for money. All the locks on these windows need to be replaced, Kelly.''

"Would you save the lecture?'' He wasn't telling her anything she didn't know.

They walked through her bedroom. Nothing had been disturbed. Ash noticed the nightgown hanging on the back of the bathroom door. It was a sheer green and it took him a long time to move past it. His reaction caused a thrill to go through her. It shouldn't have, but it did.

They next looked in the nursery. Nothing had been touched. When he met her gaze, the outside world ceased to exist for a moment. There was a sense of peace between them.

"Is Kelly here?'' Mrs. Schattle asked, her voice carrying from the front door.

"I guess we better talk to our neighbor,'' Kelly said, then realized what she had said. *Our* neighbor, as if she was Ash's, too.

"Kelly, darling, where are you?'' Mrs. Schattle called.

Kelly and Ash walked out of the nursery and back into the living room where the older woman glared at Eric. He shrugged, as if to say *what could I do?*

Mrs. Schattle had snow-white hair, coiled into a bun on the top of her head. She was under five feet, her hands knotted with arthritis and she walked slowly, but her eyes were as bright and sharp as they had been when she was twenty.

"Did that thief take much, dear?'' she asked.

"I don't know, Mrs. Schattle. Thank you for calling this in,'' Kelly answered.

The old woman beamed. "I do what I can.''

"And I appreciate it.''

Mrs. Schattle looked at Ash. "It's nice to see you again, young man." A grin creased her mouth. "It's about time you came home."

Kelly's eyes widened. Ash choked back a response. Luckily the evidence man walked into the room.

Ash pulled a picture from the inside pocket of his sport coat. "Was this the guy you saw, Mrs. Schattle?"

She squinted at the picture. "I can't say. I didn't get a good look at his face. The hair's the right color."

"Thanks." Ash smiled at the woman.

"I'm finished," Eric announced. "I'll run the prints I found and get back to you." He walked out the front door.

Kelly turned to Mrs. Schattle. "We're going to have to go through my library. Thank you again for calling this in."

"You are very welcome, my dear." She turned and left.

Three hours later, Kelly knew that no files had been taken.

"It looks like maybe our guess was right," Ash said.

"Maybe the thief was looking for something else— money stocks, and thought they might be in the library." From the expression on his face, Kelly knew her wild assumption didn't wash. "All right, it's far-fetched."

He frowned. "Maybe you should spend the night somewhere else."

"No."

"Just for tonight," he urged.

Her jaw locked and her eyes hardened. He knew that look. Dynamite wouldn't move her. "I'm not running, Ash."

His gaze narrowed, and Kelly prepared herself for the fight. After a minute, he shrugged. "Okay."

He stood and walked to the front door.

She stared. "Is that all you're going to say?" she demanded.

"Will anything I say make a difference?" he asked reasonably.

Why was he acting so cool and calm now when earlier he had acted like an avenging angel, storming into the room where she was getting a massage?

As she watched him drive away, Kelly couldn't believe he had left. What kind of police protection was that?

Ash sat in his car, watching the Procters' house. He had gone by Bruce Rhodes's apartment but the man hadn't returned, so Ash had decided to question the Procters' secretary.

Their Mercedes pulled out of the driveway and drove down the street. He didn't doubt they were going to the reception for the Houston Opera. They were big supporters.

He pushed opened his car door and walked to the mansion's front door. He rang the bell and waited. When the housekeeper opened the door, Ash flashed his badge.

"Mr. and Mrs. Procter are not here," the older woman told him.

"I didn't come to talk to them. Is Rebecca Bryant here?" It wasn't hard to discover the name of the Procters' secretary.

She quickly hid her surprise and showed him into the living room. A moment late, a woman in her thirties walked into the room. She was dressed in tailored black slacks and an elegant white blouse. Her hair was carefully styled and her earring modest. But he noticed that her top two buttons were undone.

"How can I help you, Detective?"

"Do you know if Catherine Reed ever told her parents that she wanted a divorce from her husband?"

All color drained from her face. She glanced toward the kitchen. "Could I walk you to your car?"

He understood she didn't want to be overheard. "Sure."

She walked outside with him. "Catherine told her parents she wanted a divorce the April before she died. I was doing taxes when she walked into the house. I heard the argument." She glanced at the house. "Her father told her Procters didn't divorce. And if she continued talking about it, he'd cut her off without a cent."

Ash looked Rebecca in the eye. "Why didn't you mention this to someone?"

She glanced at the house across the street. "Because I want to keep my job."

"Andrew Reed, what do you think of him?"

She looked down at her feet.

"What is it, Rebecca?"

"I was one of Andrew's conquests." She shrugged. "I was flattered that he noticed me. But when I openly flirted with him in front of the Procters, he told me I was a fool and slapped me."

"And you didn't point this out to any investigator?" Ash demanded.

"I didn't want to cross him. He told me it wouldn't be beneficial for my health if I did."

"And you believed him?"

Her eyes were stark. "Yes."

"So why tell me now?"

"Because I vowed to myself I wouldn't lie if asked."

"But not volunteer any information if not asked? That's a thin distinction."

She shrugged. "We all have to survive." She turned and walked back into the house.

Ash wondered why Ralph Lee hadn't questioned Rebecca. But then again, Ash had discovered an entire host of questions that Ralph hadn't asked.

Chapter 12

Kelly walked into her library, the Carlson file in her hand, and sat at the desk. It had been a waste to go back to work. She had gotten nothing done. The deposition that she was supposed to take had been delayed due to a witness's illness. The entire day should have just been canceled.

She opened the Carlson file and glanced through it. Why had she decided to take it with her? What had been bothering her about it? She'd been ready to walk out of the house that morning, when the urge to get it had washed over her.

That intuition Ash knew and approved of. She understood now why he would follow his gut. She'd given him grief about it when they were married, because his actions had usually resulted in headaches for the D.A.'s office. But those instincts also proved right nine times out of ten.

A car door slamming made her jerk. The doorbell

sounded. Opening the front door, she noted that Ash had a big sack from the local home-improvement store. "What are you doing?" she asked.

He gave her a dark look. He stepped back and eyed the plunger handle she'd wedged in the window frame to prevent it from being opened. "I'm here to fix your broken window lock. I'm also going to put some steel clamps on the window frames so that they can't be forced open like the one in the living room."

When she opened her mouth to respond, he shook his head.

"Don't argue. It won't do you any good." He marched past her into the room.

She frowned at his back. "I wasn't. I was going to thank you."

His look said he didn't believe her. His brow arched, then he went to work.

A warmth stole through her. "Since I can't talk you out of your mission, I guess I could feed you."

Ash glanced up from where he'd pulled out the locks from the sack. "I could use a good meal."

"Then it's a deal." Kelly went back into the kitchen and started a pot of spaghetti. When dinner was ready, she found Ash in her bedroom, putting the last of the locks on her windows.

Her heart turned over her in chest seeing him in their bedroom. If she was honest with herself, she would admit she missed him. She remembered countless times when he'd awakened her with kisses and the warm strokes of his hands. Their love life had never lacked, at least not until the end.

She'd had few dates since their divorce, but she hadn't been tempted to share anything more than a few kisses. Pushing aside the thought, she announced, "Dinner's ready."

He nodded and followed her into the kitchen. He didn't say anything but settled at the table.

Kelly braced herself. When Ash looked up, he resembled a young boy caught stealing the neighbor's mail.

"What?"

"I'm sorry about this afternoon at the massage clinic." He stared down into his plate of spaghetti. "I was crazy with worry by the time I found you. After visiting Joanna Kris in the hospital, seeing her injuries...then the suspect making bail." He ran his fingers through his hair. "You were supposed to be in court, then you weren't there..."

His words touched a hidden place in her heart. She didn't remember the last time Ash had apologized to her.

She laid her hand on his and, when his gaze met hers, she whispered, "Apology accepted."

He nodded and dug into his dinner.

"Has Joanna Kris regained consciousness, yet?" Kelly asked.

"She has. But whoever shot her got his message across. When we showed her Bruce Rhodes's picture, a guy we arrested who had a florist's overalls in his apartment—"

"Overalls?"

"We think that whoever shot Joanna may have posed as a floral delivery man since there was a vase of flowers on the piano in her living room. She said it wasn't him. None of her neighbors saw the man." He took another bite of his spaghetti. "I'm going to see her tomorrow and ask if Andrew ever hit her. I also might ask a couple of her friends about the situation."

She studied him. He had an expression that said there was a sticking point he couldn't get around.

"What's bothering you, Ash?"

He laughed. "There's a list, Kel."

"What's on it?"

"On the top of it is that picture of Joanna and Andrew at a party. It's like a sore tooth with me. I want to know where it was taken and when. I might take it with me and ask some society folks if they recognize the occasion."

She couldn't complain about his feelings. She'd just given in to hers and saved the Carlson file.

"I also talked to the Procters' personal secretary. They knew about Catherine filing for divorce from Andrew. Her father threatened to disown her if she divorced. She dropped the action."

"I guess families don't like divorce. I can't say my folks were pleased about ours." She glanced up, realizing that she had stepped into it.

He laughed. "I won't repeat what my mom said."

Silence settled between them. So neither of their families had supported their divorce.

What if—she stopped the thought cold. There was no use going back and playing the "what if" game.

"Thank you, Ash, for what you've done here at the house. I'll sleep a lot easier with those safety locks on the windows."

"I'm glad someone will," he muttered.

"What?"

"The guy who broke in didn't find what he was looking for." He broke off a piece of bread and stuffed it into his mouth.

"And what was that?" she asked carefully, knowing the answer.

His eyes narrowed. "Don't do this dance with me, Kelly. We both think whoever broke into your place was looking for the Carlson file. Since he didn't find it, there's a chance he might come back."

It irritated the stuffing out of her when he was right.

"I should spend the night." When her eyes narrowed, he added, "On the couch."

"You've done enough with the window locks. I doubt that our thief will come back here. He wouldn't be that stupid."

Ash leaned forward. "You and I both know that criminals are dumb and do stupid things on a regular basis. A good part of our success is due to their stupidity."

She knew he was worried about her, but she wouldn't be manipulated by others. "Go home, Ash. I'll be fine."

Kelly remembered those words when she heard the window frame rattle in the living room several hours later. The sound came again. Instantly she dialed 911.

After hanging up, she grabbed the tennis racket in her closet and walked into the hall. She wasn't going to cower in the bedroom. By the time she reached the living room, the intruder had moved to the dining room window. The lock broke, but the window moved up only two inches, stopping at the lock placed in the track of the window. Over the roar of her pounding blood she heard the intruder struggle with the window, but it wouldn't move.

Silently Kelly thanked Ash for installing the locks. She heard the low curse. The man moved to another window in the library.

He tried again, getting the same result.

When were the police going to arrive? By the time she wondered it, she heard the sirens in the distance.

Kelly leaned her head back against the wall, relief making her light-headed.

By the time the police unit pulled up to her address, the intruder had disappeared. She raced into her bedroom and slipped on the robe before she answered the front door.

Before the patrolmen finished looking around the house, Ash had pulled up in her driveway. He was the most welcome sight she'd seen in a long, long time. She barely stopped herself from dashing out of the house and into his arms.

After identifying himself to the officers, he opened his arms and Kelly walked into them. His heat and strength were welcome, a place of safety and comfort.

"I'm going to spend the rest of the night, Kel." His tone left no room for argument.

If he expected one, he didn't get it. It was a smart person who knew when they needed help. And she needed help. She needed him.

He pulled back and looked into her eyes.

"I might be stubborn, but I'm not a fool."

He grinned.

"The sofa's long enough for you," she added.

"I know."

"Let's talk to the officers and see what they uncovered, then maybe I can get you a cup of coffee."

"You got a deal."

They sat at the kitchen table, nursing cups of coffee. It had taken less than ten minutes to get from his apartment to Kelly's, from the time dispatch had called him with the news of Kelly's call. His dome light flashing, he'd run every light. Ash hadn't been asleep but lying awake. Twice he had almost dressed and driven to her house. He hadn't liked leaving her alone, but knew his stubborn ex-wife had made up her mind and wouldn't appreciate him overruling her.

Fear had made his heart race as if he'd run a marathon. He knew he wasn't going to leave her alone again until this case was resolved. She might not like it, but that was just too bad. What surprised him was that she didn't argue with him on the edict. Oh sure, she didn't know his staying was a long-term thing, but she'd welcomed him to stay the night. That was a sure sign of her fear.

"We need to look at the Carlson file again and see what it is that someone wants," Ash said.

"You want to do that now?" She glanced at the clock over the stove. "It's two forty-five."

"Some of my best work is done at this time of the night." He'd meant thinking, but visions of them in bed together filled his head.

Her eyes widened and he knew she was thinking the same thing.

"Finding clues," he whispered, taking pity on her.

"Why don't we try to look at the case tomorrow morning. I'll get you a pillow and some blankets." She stood and put her cup into the sink, then hurried out of the room.

He rinsed out his cup, then went into the living room. Kelly came out the bedroom with a pillow and blanket and handed them to him.

"I'll see you tomorrow."

He smiled, but every instinct was screaming at him to follow her into that bedroom. He ignored them.

* * *

She couldn't sleep. Not with Ash in the other room.
But the reason for her lack of sleep wasn't fear. It was
want. She wanted to go to him and lose herself in his
strength. Being with him these past few days, feeling
his arms around her, his lips on hers, had brought a host
of emotions with them.

And hunger.

She got up and went into the bathroom, getting a
drink of water. When she came back into the bedroom,
Ash stood there by the bed, his gun in his hand.

"I heard a noise. I was worried about you."

"I was thirsty." She tried to smile. "I sound like a
four-year-old."

He had on his jeans, but he didn't have a shirt on.
He stepped closer. "In no way do you remind me of a
child."

His chest was inches from her face. Her gaze traveled
up his throat to his chin then his wonderful lips. Her
fingers itched to touch him. "What do I remind you
of?"

His well-formed mouth lifted into a smile. She felt
his eyes move over her body.

"A temptation."

Her gaze locked with his.

"A temptation that I need to surrender to." He placed
his gun on the nightstand, then his hands caught hers
and placed them on his shoulders. He slid his arms
around her, pulling her against him. "What do you say,
Kel? Do you want to yield, too?"

"More than anything," she whispered, raising up on
her toes and meeting her mouth to his. This time they
both knew this wasn't for show, or anyone else's benefit
but their own.

It was the most welcome kiss of her life. More thrilling than the first time Ash had kissed her, because she knew the promise of that kiss, the glory.

He lifted his head and gazed into her eyes. "Do you want this, Kel? Because if you don't, tell me now and I can walk out of this room. But if you don't tell me otherwise, I intend to join you in that bed and love you."

She realized he was giving her the choice. He wouldn't try to rush her or use the pull that drove both of them. It was her choice.

She grasped his hand and led him to the bed. Her hands skimmed over his bare torso. He returned the favor by pushing the straps of her nightgown off her shoulders. The gown fell to her waist. He gazed at her.

"You're beautiful." His hands covered her breasts.

He didn't give her time to react and covered her mouth with his. He sat on the bed, pulling her into his lap. She opened her mouth, inviting him in. He didn't hesitate, but took advantage of the invitation.

His fingers slid down her neck to rest on her collarbone. His mouth followed his hand, nibbling. She ran her fingers over his shoulders and into his hair. Pulling his head up, she brought his mouth back to hers.

"Oh, you are greedy," he whispered.

She spread her fingers out and ran them over his chest. There wasn't an ounce of fat on the man.

He brushed his chest against the sensitive peaks of her breasts. She sighed.

He tumbled her onto her back and his eyes roamed over her.

"You're beautiful, Kel." His hand swept down her body, pushing off the gown. He stood, shed his pants and quickly joined her again.

She gasped at the touch of his hand. She clutched at his shoulders, urging him on.

"Don't keep torturing me, Ash."

His grin spoke of mischief. "I haven't begun, sweetheart."

He was true to his word. His hand found all the places he knew were sensitive and he made her moan with pleasure. She returned the favor and enjoyed his reaction when she bit his shoulder.

"You want to play like that?"

"No. I want you, Ash."

She didn't have to say another thing. He covered her and joined his body to hers. It was the first time in five years that she had felt whole.

Tears streamed out of the corners of her eyes.

He stopped and brushed them away. "Am I too rough?"

"No, and don't stop now. I've waited too long for this."

His strokes were sure and strong, bringing her to the edge.

"That's it, Kel. Go with it, sweetheart, go with it."

With a final thrust, he pushed her over the edge into ecstasy. He quickly followed, then collapsed on her.

"Perfect," she heard him mumble.

She shared his sentiment.

At first Ash thought he was dreaming the feel of Kelly in his arms. It took only a moment for him to realize this wasn't a dream. Kelly was lying next to him. He'd often fantasized this, but the reality was better.

He smiled into the premorning darkness.

When he had heard the sounds of movement in Kelly's room last night, he hadn't thought, he'd grabbed his weapon and charged in there, ready to defend her. When she'd come out of the bathroom, startled and in that flimsy gown, he'd been unable to move from the spot, his need for her overwhelming him.

Their lovemaking had been everything he'd remembered. She'd never been shy in her responses, nor stingy with them. Her sighs, her moans were music to his ears.

But as soon as the satisfied feeling settled, it was followed by the ugly realization of where this was going.

He didn't want to think about it. He just wanted to enjoy the moment. Enjoy the feel of her smooth skin against his, her warmth seeping into his bones. But what he really wanted was to see her smile. He slipped out of the bed, put his pants on and went into the kitchen. He'd surprise her with coffee and eggs. She always had a healthy appetite.

The smell of coffee woke Kelly, then the sound of "You've Lost that Lovin' Feelin'" floated into the room. Ash was singing.

He had a wonderful voice, deep, mellow, totally masculine. He'd been the most welcome sight last night when he had shown up, looking big and tough. Better still when she'd seen him next to her bed, gun in his hand, ready to defend her against whatever would threaten her.

Kelly stared at the ceiling. Her heart was full, but could she trust these feelings? She had trusted him before, but when she needed him, he hadn't been there.

He's not proposing, Kelly, she reminded herself.

So you're going to enjoy him without thinking of the future?

She didn't have an answer for that.

He appeared at the bedroom door with a steaming mug in his hand.

"Hey, sleepyhead. Want some coffee?" The corner of his mouth turned up with pure mischief.

"You know for a fact I'd kill for a cup," she answered.

"Bad thing to say to a cop." He strode forward, then sat on the bed next to her. "How about a kiss?" He held up the mug.

"That's a pretty steep price, but…" She propped herself up on one elbow and brushed a kiss across his lips. But what she intended as a brief kiss backfired. The taste of him was welcome, and her mouth lingered on his. When she pulled back, his eyes had a hungry quality.

"Here." He handed her the cup.

She took a sip. Gently he took the cup from her hand and set it on the nightstand.

His hands cupped the sides of her face, then he slowly lowered his mouth to hers. Kelly melted at the touch of his lips and her hands grasped his arms to anchor herself to him.

"Are you going to burn anything in the kitchen?"

He smiled. "No. I turned off the eggs before I walked in here. They'll be cold."

"But I think it will be worth it."

The humor left his face and he pushed back the hair against her cheek. "I'm glad you think so."

Kelly took another bite of the cold eggs and winced.

"I thought you said it would be worth it?" Ash teased. He stood next to her as they devoured the eggs from the frying pan still on the stove.

"It was."

He studied her. He had on only his jeans. She wore his shirt.

"But you're having second thoughts," he murmured.

"I don't know, Ash." She looked down at the counter. "I don't know."

The doorbell chimed. Ash walked into the other room.

"Hello, partner." A long silence followed. Kelly could only imagine the silent exchange that went on between the two of them. "You want some coffee?"

"Sure."

Julie and Ash appeared in the kitchen. Julie didn't blink an eyelash when she saw Kelly in Ash's shirt, didn't act as if it was an unusual thing to find him with a woman in his shirt.

"Good morning, Kelly," Julie greeted. "I was worried when I heard about your 911 call last night. When I couldn't find Ash, I decided to come over here. I'm glad everything is all right."

Kelly looked down at the pan on the stove, a blush staining her cheeks.

"So far," Ash answered before she could speak.

"Thanks for your concern." She forced a smile on her face. "I need to shower and get ready for work." She walked into the bedroom.

Julie leaned against the counter and looked at Ash. "You going to get me a cup of coffee?"

Ash pulled a cup from the cabinet and filled it.

"Thanks," she murmured when he handed it to her.

"Don't say a word," Ash cautioned. He didn't want to have to explain to anyone what had happened here. He didn't want to face it or analyze it.

"I thought you might want to see Joanna Kris. She's taken a turn for the worse."

He snapped upright. "You're right." He started out of the room when the phone rang. He picked it up. "Hello," he barked.

"I was calling Kelly Whalen," the woman said tentatively.

Ash recognized the voice of his ex-mother-in-law. "Morning, Jean."

"Ash? What are you doing—is everything okay?"

He had to smile. Jean was a very proper lady. Widowed for the past fifteen years, she'd raised her two sons and a daughter on her secretary's salary.

"I came by to talk to Kelly about a case. She's showering now, but when she gets out I'll have her call you."

She hesitated. "Thank you. It was nice to talk to you again. Come see me."

He'd been fortunate that his mother-in-law was crazy about him. Kelly's family had welcomed him. Her two brothers both worked in the oil industry in Beaumont. He hadn't seen them since the death of their child.

When he hung up, Julie pinned him with her gaze.

"I'll get dressed and we'll go see about Joanna."

He hadn't brought another shirt with him when he rushed over here last night. Walking into the bedroom, he wondered if Kelly had left his shirt on the bed. No such luck.

He knocked on the bathroom door. "Kel."

She opened the door. Wrapped in a towel, her hair wet, she looked at him.

"I need my shirt. Joanna Kris isn't doing well. Julie and I going to talk to her again."

She reached behind the door and grabbed his shirt. "Here."

He took it. "Thanks. Your mom just called."

She paled.

"She wants you to call her back."

"Terrific," she grumbled.

"What's wrong?" he asked.

Her head snapped up. "What did you say to her?"

"That I came by for some great sex with my ex-wife. Is there a problem with that?"

She laughed. "Yeah. They always wanted to know why I was so stupid to let you get away." She closed the door in his face.

Astounded at her words, he stared at the door. His parents and sister had given him no end of grief for letting Kelly go. His dad had been particularly rough, asking what he was using for brains to let *that* pretty and smart woman go. His sister hadn't been so kind.

"Ash, let's get going," Julie called.

He snapped out of his stupor. Pulling on his shirt, he wondered if he should let Kelly know he'd be back tonight.

Naw, he wouldn't warn her. He didn't have the time to argue.

When they walked into intensive care, Ash noticed that Joanna Kris's cubical was empty. He turned to the nurse at the desk and asked where she was.

"She died about twenty minutes ago."

A sense of urgency hit Ash. He looked at Julie. "We need to go over to Joanna's house and get that picture. I want to know where and when it was taken."

"Why?"

"Because I have a feeling about it."

She didn't question him, but nodded and started for the door.

* * *

"Kelly, are you all right?" Jake asked. "I just heard about the break-in."

She looked up from her desk. She had the feeling this wasn't strictly a social call. "I'm fine. But whoever broke in yesterday came back last night. Ash and I think they were after the Carlson file."

Jake closed the door and walked to her desk, settling in the chair before it. "I think you're right."

"Thank you, Jake, for your support in the face of the Procters' protests."

"I might have to eat a lot of rubber chicken, but I'm not going to compromise my honor. But I can hope that you and Ash are closing in on something that I can use to fight back. Bootlicking is an art form here, but I'd like to do some boot-kicking, too." He grinned. "I've taken it, now I want to be able to dish it out."

"We've established that Andrew Reed doesn't have an alibi for Catherine's murder. He also has a bad temper. We've uncovered a number of women who Andrew had been fooling around with. He's a modern-day Don Juan. Ash talked to the Procters' secretary and learned Catherine's parents knew she wanted a divorce. He has other avenues he wants to investigate. We must be doing something to rattle someone's cage as evidenced by the break-in at my house."

Jake nodded and stood. "Let me know when you turn up something I can use."

"You'll be the first one to know, Jake. Believe me, you'll be the first to know."

After he left the room, Kelly blew out a breath, resting her head on the back of her chair. The entire world around her was unraveling and at every turn there was trouble. And yet, what did she find herself thinking about? Ash and the way he had made love to her last night and this morning.

Did he still blame her for their daughter's death? She'd had a big case she was trying five years ago. She had run herself ragged putting it together, not eating as she should, not sleeping. They'd argued the day before the miscarriage about her not taking care of herself. What hurt the most was she feared that his accusation was true.

She pushed aside the thoughts. They needed to concentrate on this case and solve it. Period.

She didn't want anything more.

But in her heart, she knew she wasn't admitting the truth.

Chapter 13

"Detective Ashcroft, how nice to see you again," Mrs. Ackers greeted as she walked into the living room. "What can I do for you?"

Ash shook her hand. "I have a couple of follow-up questions I'd like to ask you about the night of Catherine's death."

Her smile tightened.

"This will only take a moment of your time, and I think you'd rather answer than have me question your guests."

"All right." She sat down.

"You said that Catherine and Andrew didn't exchange words after she caught him with his mistress, but you knew she was mad."

"I could see it in her eyes. I don't doubt they fought on the way home."

"When did they leave?" Ash pushed.

She frowned. "It's been so long ago. I'm not sure."

"Was it early in the evening, middle, toward the end of the party?"

"It was the middle of the party."

Ash nodded. "And when did the party break up?"

"One a.m."

He pulled Joanna's photo out of his jacket pocket and showed it to Mrs. Ackers. "Do you know when this picture was taken?"

She studied the five-by-seven photo. "It was taken the night Catherine was murdered." She pointed to her dress. "I remember wearing that dress. It was the first time I'd worn the Valtrot."

Ash frowned. "Valtrot?"

"The hottest designer in this city. It was a new dress. He also does men's clothing."

"From the smiles, this must have been taken before Catherine found her husband with his mistress."

"It was."

"Do you have any more pictures taken of that night?"

"Yes."

"Could you get them for me?" he asked.

She stood and walked into another room. She returned with a photo album. When she opened it, there were several shots of Andrew throughout the night.

"Mind if I take a couple of these?" he asked.

She gave him the photos.

Ash drove to the D.A.'s office, since he knew Kelly had the Carlson file with her. He wanted to compare pictures to see what was bothering him.

"Kelly, good, you're here." Teresa Myers stood and took Kelly's briefcase. "Mr. Thorpe wants you in his office, *now*. I'll put this away for you."

Kelly knocked on the closed door.

"Enter."

Kelly opened the door and stopped when she saw Andrew Reed standing before Jake's desk.

Andrew's eyes narrowed. "There she is. I want an explanation as to what the hell is going on? Why is that detective of hers continuing to nose around in Catherine's affairs? Do you know how upset my in-laws are that this nightmare hasn't ended? Do you let your detectives go on witch hunts whenever they feel like it? That man is a renegade, an insult to law-abiding citizens."

The pompous jerk had crossed the line. "Law-abiding citizen?" Kelly ground out. She glanced at Jake, wanting to see his reaction. He nodded for her to continue.

"Detective Ashcroft is no renegade. He's one of the best investigators in HPD. That's why he was assigned to the case. I trust him and his word. There are still questions about Catherine's murder, because I'm not satisfied that we prosecuted the right man." Her voice rose with each word. She didn't doubt the entire office had heard her defense of Ash, but that didn't matter. "And there's not a prosecutor in this office that wouldn't have him on a case."

Andrew puffed up like a toad. "So you agree with his methods?"

"I do."

"Why are you doing this?" he demanded.

She took a step toward him. "I'll tell you why. The way your wife was murdered speaks of rage, Mr. Reed. A personal rage that someone directed at your wife.

"Didn't you and your wife create a scene at the party you attended that night?"

A muscle in his jaw jumped. "That has nothing to do with my wife's murder."

"That's where you're wrong. Statistically, a murder like Catherine's is ninety-nine point nine percent of the time committed by a close acquaintance. Steve Carlson didn't do it. He might have stolen your wife's jewelry, but he didn't kill her. So we are looking at various people to see who could have directed such anger at her."

His eyes narrowed. "You're trying to pin this on me?"

If the shoe fits... "I'm trying to find your wife's murderer. I would think you'd want that."

Anger pulsed off him. "What I want is to be left alone. And my in-laws as well."

He glared at Jake and Kelly, then stormed out of the room.

Kelly turned to her boss. "I guess it was okay to let him know that we're still investigating."

Jake's brow arched. "A little late to worry about it."

"Well, he was going to learn about it sooner or later," Kelly reasoned.

"So let's slap him in the face with the information we've gathered."

Kelly folded her arms over her chest. "That's why you're the D.A. and I'm A.D.A."

He laughed and shook his head. "At this rate, you won't be running for my job for a long time. You discover anything more to implicate Mr. Reed?" Although Jake might appear to be relaxed, Kelly saw the telltale signs of his tension by the way his fingers wrapped around his pen.

"Yeah, we've discovered something to nail the bastard." Ash's voice rang through the room.

Kelly and Jake turned as Ash strolled into the room, a folder in his hand.

"What's that?" Jake asked.

Ash placed the folder on the desk, then opened it and lined up four photos. "These pictures were taken the night of the murder. These first three are during the party. Notice what Mr. Reed is wearing."

They glanced at the photos.

"Now look at the picture taken after Catherine's murder had been reported."

Kelly looked and noticed there was a slight difference in the shirt, but it was the cummerbund that was markedly different.

"He's not wearing the same thing. Of course, if you've hacked your wife to death, it's messy. He probably had to throw away his tux and change into another one. Normally it would be hard to tell the difference—a tux is a tux. But if look closely, you'll see the jackets aren't the same. Earlier, I took Andrew's photo out of the file and took it by our friends down at the tux rental place. They told me an interesting tidbit. The tux in the picture at the party is by a local designer, Valtrot. The second one is slightly different, by a different designer." He shrugged. "We need to ask Andrew where his Valtrot tux is now."

"Have you checked with the designer?" Kelly asked.

"I did, and he confirmed the man isn't wearing the same tux."

"Maybe you should pull him in for questioning," Jake suggested.

Ash smiled. "There's nothing I'd like better. Or maybe catch him out tonight and see his reaction."

"I like that idea," Kelly answered. "How's Joanna Kris?"

"She died this morning."

Kelly closed her eyes. Joanna was the third person to die in this investigation. "The body count is rising."

"Then maybe we should corner Mr. Reed tonight," Ash answered. "I doubt we'll shake him, but it will be interesting to see what he does."

"All right. If we do it before a crowd, he can't claim you coerced him."

He grinned. "I won't lay a hand on him."

Ash went back to police headquarters and filled his captain in on what had happened. "Not only are the Procters upset, but Andrew Reed is on the warpath."

"Let's see what shakes out, Ash."

"You're not mad?" Ash had expected a different reaction.

"If I understand it right, the A.D.A. was the one who dumped on Andrew Reed. The police aren't responsible for the actions of lawyers."

Ash laughed. "I've got reports to do."

"You going to include last night?"

Ash stared at his captain. He had no intention of writing up his activities. Apparently his thoughts were communicated, because Captain Jenkins laughed.

"I was referring to the break-in at the A.D.A.'s home. Nothing else."

Ash felt like a fool. "It'll be in the report."

Ash walked to his desk. Julie was in court this afternoon, and most of the day shift was out. As he wrote his report, Kelly's words that he had overheard floated back to him.

Detective Ashcroft is no renegade. He's one of the best investigators in HPD. That's why he was assigned to the case. So she thought he was a good investigator. *I trust him and his word.*

A smile creased his face. Kelly had always believed in him. She had often told him she thought he was one of the best investigators she'd ever encountered.

She'd never been stingy with her praise of him. But he couldn't say that about himself. When Kelly had needed him, he hadn't been there for her.

Could they capture the magic they had before? Did he dare take the risk? Since he'd divorced Kelly, he hadn't had a serious relationship with a woman, much to his family's displeasure. He hadn't been interested in sharing himself with any woman. Funny, Ash found himself wanting to talk to Kelly about things besides this case.

Could he risk it? Would she walk out on him again if he failed her?

"Hey, partner. What has you looking like you ate your last Snickers bar?" Julie asked as she sat down.

"I thought you were in court."

"My guy copped a plea. Took a look at the jury and decided that they weren't going to give him a break."

He nodded.

"You didn't answer my question."

"I think we've found evidence that points to Andrew Reed." He explained.

She cocked her head. "You didn't answer my question, Ash."

From her expression, he wasn't going to be able to divert his partner. "I was thinking about Kelly."

"What about her?"

Julie knew darn well what he was thinking. She'd found him and Kelly half-dressed in the kitchen, eating breakfast. "As if you don't know."

She leaned forward. "Admit it, partner."

"I want another chance with her."

A satisfied smile curved her lips. "It's about time you woke up, Ash."

He leaned back. "So you're all for it."

"You two are a great team. Although I don't know Kelly that well, I've always thought you two seemed perfect for each other."

He valued Julie's opinion.

He nodded. "Thanks for the support. I'm going to give it a try."

As Ash walked toward his car, Ralph Lee stepped into his path. "I don't appreciate you questioning my work." He bared his teeth.

"What are you talking about?" Ash wanted to hear Ralph put into words what was bothering him.

"I was just chewed out by the captain. He wondered why I didn't check out Andrew Reed's alibi."

"I wondered that myself."

Ralph's expression hardened. "I had the murderer. I didn't need to check out Andrew Reed."

Ash couldn't believe his ears. What was wrong with Ralph? "You're right." He took a step away.

"That's it?" Ralph demanded.

"You've got it." Ash felt Ralph's gaze on his back, drilling holes through him as he walked to his car. The other detective's reaction was out of line. What was it that was really bothering him?

Ash knocked on Kelly's door. He had the urge to turn around and wave to Mrs. Schattle. He heard Kelly's footsteps, then she opened the door and smiled.

"Apparently you want to give Mrs. Schattle another

show,'' he whispered as he stepped inside. He reached for her and pulled her into his arms. His lips covered hers.

It hadn't been a mistake, the memory he'd relived all day today was real. Her lips were sweeter than the finest wine he'd ever had.

His tongue slipped inside her mouth to duel with hers. Her fingers combed through his hair as she snuggled closer to him.

He rested his forehead against hers. "If you don't want to make love here in the hall, then don't wiggle like that again," he breathed.

Looking into her eyes, he saw her consider his words. A smile crossed her face. "Really?"

Her response made him smile. He was tempted to show her exactly what he meant by pinning her against the wall. Instead, he grabbed her hand and placed it over his zipper.

"Does that answer your question?"

"Yes." Her eyes softened. "I'd dare you, but I don't want either of us pulling a muscle."

"So you think I'm that old?"

"No. I think I am."

"But it would be worth it."

She shook her head. "You always liked to live on the dangerous side."

He stepped away and took a breath. There were things they needed to discuss, but it seemed that every time he was near her his brain short-circuited.

"You ready for this show tonight?" Ash asked her. They were going to catch Andrew Reed tonight at the museum gala put together by Andrew's newest fiancée.

"I need to reapply my lipstick," she murmured, brushing color from his mouth.

He grabbed her hand and gently kissed the palm. His eyes locked with hers. "We need to talk."

"About what?"

"You and me."

Her eyes widened. She glanced at her watch. "We don't have time now."

She was right. Now wasn't the time. "I plan to spend the night here, Kelly. And in your bed. It doesn't matter to me when we talk, but we'll talk. Besides, our suspect, Bruce Rhodes, is out on bail. I don't want a repeat of the other night's break-in."

She studied him for a moment. "All right. Let me get my purse, and then we'll go."

Ash watched as she hurried off. Her reaction surprised him. Didn't most women want to discuss their relationships with their men? That didn't appear to be the case with Kelly.

And exactly what he was going to say?

He wanted another chance, that's what.

Kelly's insides shook. She didn't want to talk to Ash about their relationship. Couldn't they just go on as they had been?

She walked out of the bedroom. Ash opened the front door.

"I had a run-in with Ralph Lee today, Kelly."

That worried her. Ralph wasn't an easy man to get along with. "Over what?" She slid into the front seat of his car.

"This case." He closed the door and walked around the car. "He told me the reason he didn't follow up on Andrew's alibi was that they had caught the man who killed Catherine. Well, it got me to wondering about

Ralph. I went down to records. I know one of the ladies there.''

He glanced at her. Kelly didn't doubt the woman in records gladly helped.

''She pulled Ralph's personnel file for me,'' he continued. ''It seems that he grew up in a little town north of Houston called Cut and Shoot. It was the same little town where Andrew Reed grew up.''

Kelly gaped at Ash. ''They're both from the same little town?''

''Graduated within two years of each other.''

''Then they have to know each other,'' Kelly muttered.

''I think so, too. It would be worth a trip to that little town to check it out. Can you go tomorrow?''

She thought about her cases tomorrow. ''In the morning, but I have to be back by two.''

''Then tomorrow we'll see the connection between the two men.''

''If Ralph and Andrew knew each other, then the inconsistencies of this case—''

''—make a lot of sense. There's a good reason why there was no blood evidence on Carlson's clothes.'' At the stoplight he glanced at her. ''Carlson robs the Reed home. He hears them driving up into the driveway and cuts out. Andrew and Catherine argue. They're inside the house. She probably tells him she wants to divorce him.''

''And he won't get any money, because he came into the marriage without any or because of a prenup.''

Ash pulled into the museum parking lot. ''He's developed a taste for the good life. He grabs the saber, which Carlson had taken off the wall, and hacks his wife to death. And that's why, in the pictures taken after

the murder, Andrew has on another tux.'' He turned off
the ignition. ''Should we go inside and see if we can
rattle Mr. Reed's cage?''

''Sounds good to me. You've got the pictures?''

Ash patted his suit coat.

''Then let's go.''

Soft music filled the air as well-dressed couples
preened and strutted. In the midst of the elegant crowd,
Andrew Reed and his fiancée were holding court at the
punch bowl. The man obviously enjoyed being the center of attention.

Ash stepped into the circle of people.

''Detective Ashcroft, Ms. Whalen,'' Andrew coolly
greeted them.

''We need to talk to you, Mr. Reed, to clear up some
problems we have with your wife's murder,'' Ash informed him.

A gasp ran through the crowd.

''I thought this nonsense was over,'' Andrew stated,
glancing around the gathering. ''If you want to talk to
me, you can talk to my lawyer.''

''That's true. I can haul you and your lawyer downtown to answer this question, or you can give me five
minutes of your time to answer my question.''

Andrew glared at Kelly. ''This is out of line.''

''Detective Ashcroft is being reasonable, Mr. Reed.
It seems to me you're the one who's mucking up the
process. Five minutes here or downtown. It's your
call.''

''We don't even have to move,'' Ash added. ''The
more witnesses we have, the better to insure that you're
not abused.''

Andrew's glare could have started a fire. ''Here, but

let's not involve these guests." He motioned toward the table at the back of the room.

They walked to the table tucked into a corner. Andrew's fiancée accompanied him. Once at the table, Andrew turned on Ash. "What do you want?"

Ash pulled the pictures from the inside pocket of his suit jacket and placed them on the table. Both Andrew and Michelle looked at the pictures.

The quiet in the room intensified. Andrew scanned the crowd, his jaw tightening as he understood his humiliation. He then looked at the table.

Ash waited as Andrew's gaze moved over the photos. "Can you explain to me why you changed your tux? In this photo, you have on a different coat and cummerbund than the one you wore later when the police interviewed you?"

"That's ridiculous, Detective." Michelle turned to Andrew. "Explain it to him, sweetheart." She motioned for him to dispatch the detective.

Cold, hard fury filled Andrew's eyes as he looked at Ash. "These aren't from the same night."

They had him. "They are," Ash replied. "Those photos are from the party at the Ackers." He pointed to the group of pictures taken from the party, and Joanna's photo. "I checked it out with your hostess. She validated that these pictures were taken the same night." He picked up the photo taken by the police. "This one was taken after your wife's murder by the police. I even had your tailor tell me that the tux is different."

Michelle gasped. Her expression pleading, she said, "Explain it to them, Andrew."

He pulled his shoulders back. "If the detective wants

me to answer any more questions, he'll have to direct them to my lawyer.''

Her head whipped around and she gaped at him. "What?"

He grasped his fiancée's arm and pulled her away. The crowd of people in the room parted as Andrew and Michelle moved to the door.

"I think you've ruined his party for him," Kelly whispered.

Ash picked up the pictures and tucked them back into his jacket. "That's not all I've ruined for him."

They followed Andrew and Michelle outside. The couple was nowhere to be seen.

"Why don't we walk around and see if we can find them."

She studied him. "Sounds good."

It was a beautiful night, the temperature in the low seventies, a breeze fluttering the newly blossomed trees. He grasped her hand and smiled at her when she threw him a questioning glance.

"We'll appear less threatening if we're posing as lovers."

"All right."

As they walked across the parking lot, Ash searched for any signs of Andrew and Michelle. He continued through the parking lot, down the walk that led to the concrete bayou. He scanned the area.

He stopped and pulled Kelly into his arms. "I think we've shaken Andrew Reed."

"We've also upset his fiancée. She appeared shocked."

Looking down at her, Ash smiled. "It has to be a shock to discover your husband-to-be might have killed his first wife—"

"—who had money," Kelly finished the sentence.

"I think a visit to Michelle tomorrow might prove very beneficial." His fingers combed through Kelly's hair.

Her eyes drifted closed. "Before we go to visit Andrew's hometown?"

"We could do that first." His fingers skimmed over her lips. "Why don't we go home?"

"That's a wonderful idea."

As they walked back up the path, they heard Michelle Graham. "Take me home, Andrew."

"You don't understand," Andrew hissed, grabbing her arm and forcing her to face him. "That cop has always been after me. They're trying to frame me."

Ash and Kelly walked out of the trees by the parking lot. Michelle looked at them.

"Why are you doing this?" Michelle asked them.

"Because of the unanswered questions," Ash replied. "And the murder of the man accused of the deed."

Michelle looked at Andrew. "Explain to me about the pictures, again."

He glared at her.

Michelle jerked out of his hold and ran back into the building. Andrew turned and scowled at them. Ash tensed, waiting for the other man to spring. After a long moment, Andrew followed his fiancée.

"I think Andrew ran into a major chuckhole in the road to happily-ever-after," Kelly whispered.

"And maybe we've saved Michelle's life."

Kelly instantly sobered.

Cupping her cheek, Ash asked, "Why don't we let the happy couple stew while we go home? I definitely have some ideas of what we can do."

"You never did lack imagination, Ash."

Chapter 14

The sexual tension between Ash and Kelly escalated during the long drive home. Ash pulled his car into the driveway of Kelly's house.

She smiled at him. "What time do you want to start tomorrow?"

Oh no, she wasn't going to get away with pretending nothing was going on between them. Ash wanted her to acknowledge the awareness they shared. Facing her, he murmured, "I doubt we'll sleep later than seven. We can leave after breakfast."

"You really plan to spend the night?"

"I don't plan on running off afterward, Kel."

She blushed and turned away.

"I'm bunking here until we nail Andrew Reed. Also, I want to know where Bruce Rhodes is."

"Ah." She nodded and climbed out of the car. He had to run to catch up with her. He followed her into the hall of the house. Before she could put the keys down, he pulled her into his arms. His lips descended on hers. After an instant of hesitation, she returned his passion.

He didn't pretend to understand what went through her mind, but at this point all that mattered was that she wanted this as much as he did.

She pulled at his shirt as he shucked his suit coat. His tie got caught in the shirt. Their hands tangled as they tried to slide the knot out of the tie. Their laughter erupted.

"I'll go for the tie," he panted.

She grinned. "Okay, I'll start on the belt."

He didn't have a problem with that.

It took less than a minute for him to discard the rest of his clothes. She smiled and her fingers ran over his chest.

"You've always been a beautiful man," she breathed.

"That's our secret," he told her as his hands worked on the buttons of her blouse.

"I don't kiss and tell," she answered.

"For which I'm grateful. If any of the other detectives heard you, I'd never live it down."

He peeled the blouse down her arms, then it joined his clothes on the floor. Her skirt, shoes and underwear quickly followed.

He pulled her into his arms and carried her to the bedroom. Laying her down on the bed, he stepped back to drink in his fill.

"Do you know how often I've dreamed of this?" he whispered as he settled beside her.

Her hand cupped his cheek. After a long pause, she whispered, "Make love to me Ash."

Those words wrapped around his heart. He loved her.

Had loved her from the minute he had set eyes on her. And he wanted a future with her. But he saw a wariness in her eyes and it sparked a need in him to drive her demons away.

He tasted her, nibbling the delicate skin behind her ear and under her chin. Her moan of delight urged him on. He worked his way down to her breasts. He kissed those sweet orbs, laving each with his attention.

Kelly's hands flexed on him as the tension in her built, then she pushed him to his back. Rising up on her elbow, she smiled down at him. "I think I want to be the one in control."

He loved the look in her eyes. "I'm all yours," he whispered.

"I like that."

She started with his lips, nipping and tasting. Then she moved down his neck and lightly bit the skin at the base of his neck. Her hands skimmed over his chest.

"You've been working out," she said as her hands molded over his abdomen.

He had the time, since his social life had sucked.

Her hands moved lower, lightly cupping him. Her smile of satisfaction made him want to return the favor. His hands slid up her back to cushion her head. He urged her mouth to his. She melted over him. He eased into her and she closed her eyes and sighed. They belonged together in spite of their differences.

"Look at me, Kelly."

Her eyes fluttered open and her gaze locked with his. His hands framed her face. He didn't say anything, but with his body, he tried to let her know what was in his heart.

With each move of her body, he could see her reaction. The pleasure built and built until they both exploded in a shower of delight.

Her eyes drifted closed and she collapsed on top of him. They were parts of one whole.

When she slid off him, he gathered her into his arms. He wanted to talk to her, but instead he relaxed into the peace of holding her. As he fell asleep, Ash felt as if he'd put to rest Kelly's demons for the time being. But he knew one night of loving didn't solve all their problems. She still had doubts. He prayed he could find a way to banish those fears for good.

Kelly slipped out of bed, pulled on her robe and walked into the dining room, where she could see her garden. She'd immersed herself in her plants after the miscarriage and divorce, caring for them when she couldn't care for the child she'd lost. Here, where she could feel the earth in her hands and feel the connection to life, she'd worked out the pain in her heart.

She was shaken by what she'd seen in Ash's eyes tonight. She'd seen forever. He wanted a future with her.

She hadn't let her mind wander in that direction, but she'd better think about it now. Did she want forever-after? Could she risk her heart again? After the miscarriage, Ash had pulled away from her, leaving her to find her way through it by herself. It had taken a long time, but she'd made it. Could she risk her heart again? Take that gamble?

Maybe she was wrong and had misread the situation.

"What are you doing?" he quietly asked.

She turned. "I couldn't sleep."

He hadn't dressed and, in the moonlight, he resembled a beautiful marble statue, his chest and abdomen a sculpted masterpiece. His gaze searched her face. "Why?"

Needing to face the situation, she said, "I was thinking about us."

His face lightened and he pulled her into his arms. "What were you thinking?" His fingers pushed back the strand of hair that had drifted onto her cheek.

"I was wondering where we're going."

"You know what I want? I want us to be a team like we've been on this case. We're good together, Kel, we know how each other operates. And what we share in bed—" he grinned "—is special. I want us to get married again."

She couldn't look at him anymore. Her gaze focused on his chest.

"I take it you don't feel that way."

How could she explain this fear that had settled into a hard knot in her stomach. "I'm afraid, Ash."

His fingers lifted her chin. "Of what?"

"Of trusting you again."

Like a bullet, her doubt hit its mark, wounding him. His arms fell away and he took a step back.

"I thought we had laid that ghost to rest."

"When?"

"Days ago when you cried in my arms."

She frowned at him. "Oh, there was some relief, but that didn't answer my questions, Ash. Why didn't you talk to me, hold me after I lost the baby? I was so alone and in pain and you ignored me, walked away."

"I walked away?" Anger sparked in his gaze. "As I recall, I tried, but you told me you wanted to be left alone."

Kelly remembered that night. They had fought. He had told her that if she hadn't been so committed to obtaining the conviction of a local drug lord, she might not have lost the baby. It had hit a nerve, because she had wondered the same thing.

"I was drowning. I needed you."

He looked away, but not before she saw a muscle jump in his clenched jaw. "I was drowning too, Kel."

He was right. She'd seen the tears he'd cried the other day. She'd never considered that before.

His fingers touched her chin, forcing her gaze to meet his. He searched her eyes, then stepped away.

She knew he wanted a response from her, an answer. But her heart couldn't give it.

"I'll spend the rest of the night on the couch." He turned and walked into the bedroom. A moment later, he reappeared with a pillow and blanket. She wanted to go to him, but her fear held her back.

She turned and gazed out into the night as if there were answers in the garden. All she found were questions. And doubts.

Ash poured water into the top of the coffeemaker. He'd taken a gamble and, at this point, didn't know if it would pay off. Kelly hadn't responded in the manner he had wished. She was still fearful of trusting him.

Could he blame her? If he were honest, he had to share in the blame of their breakup.

What was he going to do now?

He heard her footsteps in the hall. When she appeared, she was dressed in slacks and sweater. The tension around her eyes told him she hadn't slept any better last night than he.

"The bathroom's empty if you want to shower and shave. I'll fix some tomato and spaghetti soup while you're getting ready."

The first time she'd made that for breakfast, Ash had stared at it as if it was an alien concoction. But he'd tasted it and fallen in love with it. Kelly would make it for him on the weekends when they both had time. Maybe, in her own way, it was a peace offering. He nodded.

"Let me get a cup of coffee, first." After pouring himself a cup, he took a sip. He needed the jolt. "I'll only be ten minutes."

She grinned at his reaction and, for an instant, they connected.

He wanted that connection to be permanent. Did she?

Ash and Kelly were shown into the formal living room of the Graham mansion. Michelle and her mother walked in minutes later and sat on the opposite couch.

"We're sorry to disturb you, Michelle, but we wanted to talk to you," Kelly began.

The young woman sighed and stared down at her hands. "You'll be glad to know I broke off the engagement with Andrew last night."

Kelly glanced at Ash. "Why is that?"

When her gaze lifted, tears glistened in her eyes. "I asked Andrew to explain about the tux. He refused, claimed I didn't love him if I'd ask him something like that." She sniffed. "I told him that if he loved me he'd answer my question. He wouldn't, and the look he gave me made my blood run cold, so I gave him back his ring. He took it and drove me home."

"It's all right, sweetheart," Michelle's mother whispered, pulling her daughter into her arms. "There have been rumors about him."

"What rumors are you talking about?" Ash questioned.

"That Andrew is in financial trouble."

"Where did you hear that, Mrs. Graham?" he pressed.

"My husband's banker. He is also Andrew's. He mentioned it casually in passing one day. I worried about it, but Michelle seemed so much in love and Andrew has always been such a gentleman. I ignored the report."

Michelle glared at Ash. "Why did you bring those pictures to the reception? Why couldn't you have waited?"

"Because, Michelle," Kelly answered, "both Detective Ashcroft and I believe that Andrew murdered his wife. You needed to know that about him."

"I'll be the talk of this town," Michelle complained.

"Maybe, but people will realize you did the right thing," Kelly offered.

"And when he's convicted of murder, you'll be glad not to be married to him," Ash added.

They quickly left.

"I think the pressure on Andrew has been upped a notch," Ash said as they drove away.

"You're right." Kelly shook her head. "Girls like Michelle aren't used to having their wills thwarted," Kelly replied. "But to be fair to her, any young woman would be upset to discover her fiancé was a murderer."

He glanced at her and grinned. "You have a point. Murder tends to put some girls out of the mood."

Cut and Shoot, Texas, was a widening in the two-lane road in the piney woods. It was made up of a grocery-feed store, gas station-garage and a post office.

Ash stopped at the post office, and after identifying himself as a Houston cop, he asked, "Is there someone around here who can answer some questions about your city?''

The postmaster rubbed his chin. ''I've worked at this here post office for the past two years. Maud Lyon has been here all her life. She can answer all your questions.'' He gave them directions to the house buried back in the thick woods.

After fifteen minutes of negotiating the single dirt road, they arrived at Maud's tiny house. It was a well-kept frame home, with a large garden to the side of the house.

The woman on her knees among the iris looked up when they stopped. Her gray hair was pulled back into a ponytail.

''What can I do for you folks?'' she asked, rising.

Ash introduced himself and Kelly and told the older woman why they were here.

''Let's sit on the porch and you tell me what you want to know.''

They followed the woman to the wicker chairs by the front door.

''Do you remember a man name Andrew Reed?'' Ash inquired.

''I do. His mama grew up in this here town. Pretty little thing she was. She married Marvin Lee. Marv was a pretty talker, but worthless as spit. Carol put up with his shenanigans for a couple of years, then one day up and left town, leaving her oldest boy with that drunk.'' She closed her eyes and sighed.

''She come back about three years later, Andrew in tow. She claimed Andrew was her boyfriend's child, but he called her momma.''

''She wasn't the mother?'' Kelly asked.

''She denied it.'' The woman shrugged. ''Now where

was I? Oh, yes, Marvin was sick, dying from all that drink. He passed. Carol left the boys with her sister and lit out again. She often wandered back into town with another man. The last time she came to town, the man she'd hooked up with was real slick. He married her. Andrew took his last name. She died in a boating accident. I heard that old boy got a lot of money from that accident.''

Ash had a premonition. ''You said that she had an older son. What was his name?''

The woman looked up. ''Ralph.''

Kelly's eyes widened.

''Her sister died last year. Both the boys came for the funeral. We're all so proud of them, both of them so successful. Ralph is a police officer, just like you. And Andrew has made it big in Houston.''

The world suddenly tilted on its axis. Motives were clear and evident.

''Do you know,'' Maud continued, ''when I talked to Andrew at the funeral, asked him if he ever ran into his stepfather there in Houston, he told me that man had been shot in a robbery years ago.''

Ash's gaze met Kelly's.

''Odd how things work out,'' Maud commented.

''It is indeed,'' Kelly said.

''What was Andrew's stepfather's name?'' Ash inquired.

''Bob Reed.''

Kelly nodded. ''Thank you for you help.''

''If you need any other information, let me know.''

Ash shook the woman's hand. ''Maud, you've been more help than you'll ever know.''

The older woman smiled.

Ash's mind raced as they got back into the car.

"They're stepbrothers," Kelly said.

"Appears so," Ash said as he put the car into gear.

"And who better to help you cover up a murder than a homicide detective?" She shook her head. "But we're going to need more hard evidence that they conspired on this."

He glanced at her. "Why don't we look up the homicide of Bob Reed to see if maybe we have multiple murders."

She rested her head on the back of the seat.

"You know, Kelly, when we first started this case you asked me about Ralph's closure rate. It's made me wonder. I want to ask about his cases. Maybe he's given them a little help."

Kelly's eyes widened. "You don't think that he's made up evidence, do you?"

Ash's mouth tightened. "I don't know. But it's a nightmare scenario, and if it's true, we're going to find out." One truth he didn't look forward to discovering.

They drove to HPD headquarters and parked in the nearly empty police lot. Records had only one attendant working.

The man gave them a puzzled look. "Why don't you access the information from Homicide?"

"There's another detective using the terminal. And the A.D.A. here wanted to check the information now."

He shrugged and walked away. Kelly and Ash sat before the terminal and entered in the name of the victim. Bob Reed came up. The man had been killed in what was thought to be a robbery a week to the day after Catherine Reed died. The killer had never been caught. Both Ash and Kelly stared at the name of the investigating detective. Ralph Lee.

Kelly leaned back against the chair. "Why am I not surprised that Ralph was in on this case?"

Ash finished looking through the file. He stood and asked the clerk to see the physical file. While they waited for the file, Kelly called her office to postpone the afternoon deposition she was schedule do take.

It took fifteen minutes for the man to locate it. As they looked through it, they discovered that Ralph had claimed to be in the neighborhood when his beeper had gone off. His partner at the time had been in the hospital, recovering from food poisoning.

"Why don't we talk to Ralph's partner?" Ash asked.

"All right."

It took less than forty-five minutes to drive to the small house on the beach in Galveston.

Thomas Monteicellie was a tall man with a full head of white hair. He greeted them with a smile. "It was good to hear from you, Ash. What can I do for you?"

"I have a question on a case that Ralph had while you were in the hospital for food poisoning."

"Shoot."

"A man named Bob Reed was murdered. Ralph responded to the call since he was down there visiting you. Do you know anything about the case? Did he ever mention it to you?"

Thomas frowned. "I don't remember anything about it, but you say that Ralph was visiting me?"

"He claimed that's why he was near the crime scene and responded."

"When was this?"

"It was on the eighth of February."

"That's odd. I think I left the hospital on the seventh. Let me check." He looked through his desk and pulled out a folder of insurance papers. "Yup. I left on the seventh."

More things fell into place. Ash stood. "Thanks for your help, Tom."

"Is that all?"

"It tells me all I need to know."

Tom's eyes narrowed. "What's this about, Ash?"

"We're just trying to clear up a couple of old cases," Ash offered.

"I was curious about this murder," Kelly explained. "It seemed to be connected with another murder that I've prosecuted. I had some questions. Ash thought you'd be a good source."

"Why not ask Ralph?" Tom questioned.

"I thought you might remember something different," Kelly answered.

From Tom's expression, Ash knew they hadn't fooled the man. He didn't doubt Tom would call his ex-partner. They quickly left. As they traveled back into Houston, Ash worried.

"We didn't fool him, did we?" Kelly asked.

"Nope. I need to call my captain and let him know."

Kelly pulled out her cell phone. "What's his number?" Ash gave her the number and she dialed it, then handed it to him.

The answering machine picked up. "Captain Jenkins, we think we've found a connection between Ralph Lee and Andrew Reed. I'll give you a call later to fill you in on the information."

Ash handed her the phone.

"He killed his stepfather, didn't he?" she quietly asked.

"Or had it done, but I don't know if we'll be able to prove it."

She shook her head. "Two stepbrothers and four murders. What's going on, Ash?"

"We may have a serial killer. Or a man who killed, then tried to cover his tracks."

"I'll buy that Andrew's trying to save his rear."

Ash glanced at her. "Well, we're going to prove it, Kelly, come hell or high water."

Chapter 15

When they arrived at her house, the answering machine was blinking. Kelly played the message.

"I have information on the death of Catherine Reed—what happened to Andrew's tux," a female said without identifying herself. "Meet me at the Railhead Saloon at five this afternoon. Come alone. I'll be waiting for you behind the building."

Kelly looked at Ash. "The caller didn't identify herself, but she knew about the tux."

Ash ran his fingers through his hair. "I don't like it, Kelly. It smells to me."

"It does to me, too. But the woman knows something that could point a finger at Andrew." She glanced at her watch. "We've got less than fifteen minutes to get there."

"Let me notify Julie." He dialed HPD and talked to his partner, asking for backup.

The bar the woman named was off the freeway in

the southern, industrial area of the city. Plenty of murders happened in that rough section. It was early enough in the evening that the part-time drinkers hadn't arrived yet. Beside the bar was an X-rated video shop.

"You need to call vice down here," Kelly said as they waited for their backup.

Julie arrived, and a patrol car followed her. Ash nodded to them, then drove around to the back of the bar. Shadows from the fading sun colored the area with light and darkness. Ash parked the car and got out to see if there was anyone there. He looked behind the Dumpster and boxes, but saw no one.

He turned to Kelly. "Radio Julie. Tell her it's clear."

After the patrol car had left, Julie looked at Ash and Kelly. "You think it was a setup?" she asked.

"Sure it was," Ash answered. "The question is why? What did the caller want?"

"Maybe we should go inside and grab a drink," Kelly suggested. "Our informant might be in there."

Kelly had a point, but he didn't want to go on a stakeout with her. "Let me take you home—"

"Ash, I'm going."

He didn't like it, but Kelly walked around the front of the building, not leaving him any choice. He followed her inside.

He felt Kelly hesitate when she opened the door and the smoke and odor of stale bodies washed over them. She threw her shoulders back, then walked into the dimly lit room. Julie followed them to a table in the corner.

The waitress, a large woman with flaming red hair and a bowling shirt, appeared and took their order. There wasn't another single woman in the entire bar.

"Well, it appears that our informant isn't here," Kelly murmured into her beer.

Ash surveyed the room. Several men glanced their way, sizing up the women. Ash didn't worry about his partner, knowing she could take care of herself. It was Kelly he wanted to protect. He moved closer to her.

As they nursed their beers, Kelly told Julie what they had discovered during the day.

Julie and Ash traded a look.

"It doesn't look good for Ralph," Julie murmured.

"No, it doesn't. And things are going to hit the fan when I talk to Captain Jenkins," Ash murmured.

For close to an hour they waited, and then finally gave up and left.

"Do you suppose our caller got cold feet?" Kelly asked.

He shrugged. "Something's wrong, Kel. I just don't know what yet."

He discovered what when they opened the door to Kelly's house and stepped inside. They walked down the dark hallway to the living room. Kelly leaned over and turned on the light on the end table. Ralph sat on the couch, his gun in his hand.

"I was wondering when you two would return."

Kelly glared at him. "You sent us on that wild-goose chase."

Ralph smiled. "It seems that you two have questions you want to ask me."

Ash eyed Kelly. "We do."

"Well, before we chat, Ashcroft, hand over your service revolver," Ralph ordered.

Ash hesitated. Ralph stood, caught Kelly by the arm and jammed his gun into her side. "You don't want her hurt, do you?"

Grinding his teeth, Ash reached for the gun clipped to his belt. Ralph slid it into his jacket pocket.

"Why don't we take a little drive? We'll take your car, Ashcroft."

Ash wanted to rip the gun out of Ralph's hand, but the other detective wrapped his arm around Kelly's upper arm. "Let's go."

When they walked out of the house, Kelly glanced at her neighbor's house, praying that Mrs. Schattle was watching.

"Kelly, why don't you get into the back seat with me. Ash, you're going to drive."

Ash wondered if he could disarm Ralph, but the detective shook his head and aimed his pistol at Kelly's head.

"You could try to overpower me, but her chances of surviving won't be good," Ralph taunted.

Ash didn't want to risk Kelly's life. He stepped back. "Do what he says, Kelly."

Ash saw the mutiny on her beautiful face. He worried that she might try to bring Ralph down and tried to silently communicate for her to cooperate. If she attacked Ralph, he couldn't get to the man before he could kill her. She opened the car door, then slid inside, much to Ash's relief. Ralph followed her. He looked up at Ash. "Get in and drive."

Ash walked around the car and got behind the steering wheel.

"Get on the freeway and head south. To the ship channel."

Ash nodded and started the car.

"Now, you had questions," Ralph began.

Kelly glared at him. "Why didn't you excuse yourself from the murder investigation into Catherine Reed's murder since it was your stepbrother who was under suspicion?''

Ralph gaze hardened. "My, my, you two have been busy little bees. Few people know about Andrew's and my relationship.''

Ash glanced in the rearview mirror, wanting to see Ralph's expression.

The older detective's eyes narrowed. "If you hadn't been so determined to nail Andrew, things would've died down and gone away.''

"So you're defending what he did to his wife?'' Kelly asked, her incredulity ringing in Ash's ears.

Don't push him, Ash silently urged Kelly. She met his gaze in the mirror. He tried to communicate that message to her, but she ignored him.

"It was that or let my brother go to prison or maybe the death house,'' Ralph replied.

"Your brother?'' Kelly's surprise echoed through the car.

Everything clicked into place for Ash. The reason Ralph had gone to bat for Andrew. The blood thing proved to be true again.

"Andrew didn't deserve what he got from our mother. She was a selfish bitch who only thought of how to make her life better. Andrew always knew he was just an inconvenience for her. She never let anyone know that Andrew was hers. But we knew, Andrew and me.'' Ralph shook his head.

"Andrew loved her. And when she was murdered by our stepfather, he grieved. He became determined that he would never be a victim again.''

"So murdering his wife was okay?'' Kelly pressed.

"You don't know jack about what we went

through." Ralph glared at her. "I wasn't going to desert him like our mother did."

"Murder is never excusable," Kelly answered.

"You've both been pains in the butt," Ralph growled.

"What about your stepfather?" Kelly pressed. "Did Andrew murder him, too?"

"You don't know when to shut up, do you? I can understand why your ex divorced you."

Ash wanted to rip the detective's head off. Kelly's persistence and dogged determination were two of the things he admired about her.

"You're pretty macho, Ralph, with that gun aimed at Kelly," Ash ground out. "You want to go one on one and see how far you can get with me?"

Ralph's eyes narrowed. "Don't tempt me, Ashcroft. When the time is right, I'll enjoy taking you down several notches. Exit here."

"So you've decided to add another murder to your crime spree?" Kelly asked.

Ash's mind worked at a feverish pace as he turned onto the road to the ship channel. He watched for another police cruiser that he could signal. Nothing appeared.

"Drive to the end of the pier five," Ralph commanded.

Darkness shrouded the metal warehouses lining the dock, with an occasional light to pierce the blackness. The deserted area reminded Ash of a graveyard, and he prayed it wouldn't be theirs. Barrels were piled on one end of the dock, but there were no cars anywhere.

"Park at the end of the next building under the light," Ralph ordered.

That was the only light in the area. Ash stopped the car in front of the side door.

"Get out, both of you," Ralph ordered. Once they were out, he motioned with the gun. "Inside."

Ash glanced around the area, wanting to see the setup of the dock, looking for methods of escape. He opened the door. Kelly and Ralph followed him inside. Ralph flipped the light by the door, illuminating the partially empty warehouse.

"Over there," Ralph ordered, pointing to the front corner where several wooden crates and barrels sat.

Kelly and Ash settled on one. Ash glanced at her, trying to reassure her they would survive this. When he reached for her, Ralph shook his head.

"Move apart." He studied Ash. "Park it, Ashcroft, on the floor at her feet."

Ash hesitated.

Ralph aimed at Kelly's leg. "I can shoot her in the leg and you can watch her suffer."

Ash glared at the man, then sat on the floor.

"Now wrap your arms around her legs," Ralph commanded.

Ash complied.

"Good. This way it's harder for you to spring to your feet."

"What do you plan to do with us?" Ash asked.

"When Andrew joins us, we're going to take a little trip."

"From which we're not coming back," Kelly interjected.

"You'll be joining Bruce, who's in that barrel beside you. It will look like he was the one who killed you, then had an accident himself."

"How can you excuse what Andrew did?" Kelly demanded. "You're a cop, been sworn to uphold the law. How can you ignore what happened? Not only did he murder his wife, but your stepfather."

"When Andrew and I were kids, we were all we had. We made it through some rough times together. I couldn't desert him now." The obvious conflict inside Ralph shone in his eyes. "I can't turn my back on him."

"That's good to know," Andrew said as he walked into the warehouse.

They turned to see Andrew closing the door behind him. The look he gave both Ash and Kelly spoke of his hatred.

"What took you so long?" Ralph questioned, his mouth in a hard line.

"I've been trying to convince the little twit I was engaged to that these two were simply after me. That I didn't kill Catherine."

"And did she believe you?" Kelly asked.

Andrew glared at her. "I believe I convinced her."

"Are you going to murder this wife after she serves her purpose?" Kelly pressed.

Ash squeezed Kelly's leg, hoping to stop her from goading Andrew.

"Only if she threatens to divorce me. It wasn't very understanding of Catherine to object to my little liaisons. She was such a prude. I offered to make it a ménage à trois. She reacted poorly." He shrugged. "I hope Michelle is more adventurous."

Ash stared at Ralph. "You excuse him?"

Andrew kicked Ash. When Ash felt Kelly move toward Andrew, he held her back.

"Let's do this," Andrew growled. There was death in Andrew's eyes.

And madness.

"So who do you plan on killing first, Andrew? Or are you going to let your brother do it for you? To clean up your mess again," Kelly taunted.

Andrew darted forward and slapped Kelly across the face. Ash launched himself at Andrew, knocking him into his brother. Ash rolled to his knees and scrambled to his feet. Ralph staggered backward. Before he could regain his balance, Ash barreled into him. They both went down.

Once Andrew had his balance, he turned toward Ash and Ralph. But before he could strike out, Kelly sprang to her feet. With a well-placed kick to the back of Andrew's leg, she took him down. She quickly kneeled on his back and grabbed a hank of his hair.

Andrew yelled like a stuffed pig. "Get off me, bit—"

Ash ran Ralph into the wall, knocking the breath out of him. Ash rammed Ralph's hand into the wall several times until Ralph released the gun. With one final punch to Ralph's jaw, Ash knocked out the older man.

Sirens filled the air.

Ash retrieved the gun, ready to take on Andrew. When he turned to Kelly and saw her kneeling on Andrew's back, having him hooked like a fish, he grinned at her. "You can release Andrew's head."

When she hesitated, he laughed.

She released Andrew's hair and stood.

"I want to warn you, Andrew," Ash warned when the man started to move, "I've got the gun and won't hesitate to use it."

Kelly stepped to Ash's side.

"You're good, Kel. Damn good."

The outside door flew open and several patrolmen

rushed into the building, followed by Julie and another detective.

Julie stopped and smiled. "So you've got it under control? And your neighbor was sure you'd been kidnapped."

Ash glanced down at Kelly. "We were, but Andrew and Ralph didn't know who they were dealing with. We're a good team."

Kelly and Ash sat in Captain Jenkins's office. Jake Thorpe occupied the chair next to Kelly's.

"I don't believe it," Jake sighed.

"It is rather hard to take in," Ash commented. "I think Ralph felt guilty about his brother. He wanted to make it up to him for the lousy childhood they had."

"There are a lot of ways to compensate a sibling without covering up their tendency to murder."

Captain Jenkins shook his head. "I don't understand it. Ralph was such a good cop."

"Maybe too good," Kelly replied.

Captain Jenkins sighed. "I suppose you're going to want copies of the cases that he was the lead officer on."

Kelly glanced at her boss, silently asking him if he'd back her up on this call. He nodded. "I wish we could ignore it, Captain Jenkins. But we can't."

"I'll have those cases pulled and a list sent to your office."

She nodded and stood. She wanted to talk to Ash, wanted to share her relief about what had just happened. But they both had loose ends to attend to. Jake joined her. As they walked down the hall to the elevator, he shook his head.

"Who'd have thought such a thing could happened."

Kelly was thinking of something entirely different. Her mind was on Ash. "I didn't."

"Andrew Reed, murderer, maybe a serial killer."

Kelly came out of her haze. "Andrew?"

The elevator doors opened and they walked inside. "Yeah—Andrew. Who'd you think I was talking about?"

She blushed.

Jake's eyes widened, then he smiled. "You know, you and Detective Ashcroft are a pretty dynamic team. I think I should assign you two to some other problem cases I have. Think you could do as good?"

She looked into her boss's eyes. She knew what he was asking in his own way. Did she want to continue with Ash?

"I do think we'd make a good team. I just don't know if he will want to be permanently taken out of Homicide to work in the D.A.'s office."

Jake smiled. "Don't sweat it, Kelly."

"You look like a starving man, Ash," Captain Jenkins commented as Kelly and Jake walked out of Homicide.

Ash turned to his captain. "Not much of a poker face, huh?" He settled back into the chair he'd been sitting in.

"Nope. I see right through you."

"Too bad she doesn't."

"Don't give up, Detective. I think I saw something in the A.D.A. that makes me suspicious."

Ash sat up.

"Your powers of observation are a little off. Go for it," Jenkins encouraged.

Ash nodded and walked out of the office. Julie sat at

their desk, writing up a summary of the collar. She paused and grinned at him.

"I felt we wasted all that man power storming the warehouse only to find you and Kelly standing over Ralph and Andrew like trophies." She shook her head. "This is going to talked about for a long time."

Ash had to smile. "Some of those patrol cops did have an odd look on their faces."

"Write up your report, so you can get out of here and go home." *To your wife.* She didn't say it, but he saw it in her eyes.

Julie's words echoed Captain Jenkins's. Maybe they both saw something he hadn't. As they had sat together in the empty warehouse, Ash had admitted to himself that Kelly's complaint that he'd withdrawn from her had been valid. He hadn't pressed the point after the miscarriage because of his own grief. Alone, each of them had drowned in sorrow. Together, they would have got through it. He needed to tell her it would be different this time. She could count on him.

The question was, would she believe him?

Kelly tried to unlock the front door, then realized it had never been relocked. The day had seemed endless. A marathon.

She didn't turn on any lights, but walked into the living room and collapsed onto the sofa. Under her rear, the sofa was lumpy. She reached for the blanket under her. Ash had slept here last night.

He'd asked her to marry him, again, and she hadn't answered, frozen in her fear. But as they'd driven through the city at gunpoint, she realized how fragile life was. And how foolish she was not to grab the joy and friendship that Ash offered.

When they were at police headquarters, she had wanted to grab him and tell him that she loved him. But there hadn't been an opportunity.

Had she blown it? Did he still want to marry her?

She pulled the blanket into her lap and inhaled his scent. She closed her eyes and slipped into a peaceful sleep.

Ash knocked on Kelly's door. It was close to one in the morning. He should have waited for a more civilized hour, but he couldn't go home without settling this with Kelly.

He knocked again. Nothing.

He stepped to the window and glanced inside. When he saw Kelly slumped on the sofa, his blood ran cold.

He ran back to the front door and tried the door. When it opened, his heart nearly stopped. He raced into the living room and was on his knees in front of her, his hands roaming over her. He wanted to see where she'd been wounded.

Kelly's eyes flew open and she smiled. "What exactly are you doing?"

Ash sat back on his heels. "I'm checking for injuries."

"Injuries?"

"You didn't answer the door and, when I went to the window, I saw you slumped here and thought…" He felt like a fool. He started to get up, but her hands on his shoulders stopped him.

"Thank you, Ash, for caring."

He shrugged.

She scooted to the edge of the cushion and slipped her arms around his neck. That got his attention. His gaze met hers.

"I've been a fool, Detective. I've been afraid of ghosts. This afternoon, I knew it and prayed it wasn't too late to tell you. You are marvelous and I love you." Her eyes sparkled in the darkness. "If you still want to marry me, I'll gladly accept."

He cupped her face. "Kel, you were right. I wasn't there for you, but I can promise you that in the future I will be. It won't be perfect, but I won't shut you out."

She smiled. "That's all I ask."

He pulled her into his arms. Her weight pulled him off balance and they tumbled onto the floor.

Lying beside her, he rose up on one elbow. "I love you, Kelly, and yes I want to marry you."

Joy radiated from her. "How fast can we do it?"

"Want to run away and do Vegas? Or you want to do it here?"

"I think I want all our friends to be there. And our family, if we want them to ever speak to us again."

He brushed a kiss across her lips. "Okay, tomorrow we'll set the wheels in motion. Now let me show you how much I love you."

He paused. "And Kel, you've got to start locking the door. This is the second time I've found it open."

She smiled. "With you here, there won't be a problem."

Epilogue

Ash surveyed the crowd milling around his backyard. Nearly everyone in Homicide and the D.A.'s office had shown up for the wedding, along with their families. And Mrs. Schattle.

They'd been married by a close friend, a judge Kelly worked with. The past four days had been a sea of activity. Blood tests, licenses, calls to family and friends.

"Who would have thought this many folks would turn out to see you say 'I do' again?" Matthew Hawkins commented.

Grinning, Ash shook his head. "I never would have thought so, not after having to arrest a fellow detective."

"You were probably silently cheered. Ralph didn't have a lot of support, as evidenced by this crowd."

A good point. When Ash had announced that he was marrying again, and invited the unit, he hadn't expected this big a crowd. In addition, a good number of lawyers from the D.A.'s office had come.

"Emory laughed his head off when I told him where I was going," Hawk commented. "He said he knew you were bagged when he saw you and Kelly at the fund-raiser at his house. As a matter of fact, Edna May Vanderslice was with him. She said for me to tell Kelly she was glad the girl took her advice and captured you."

Ash's eyes widened. "So I was targeted."

"Appears so."

Kelly walked toward him, a vision in her flowing pale blue dress. When she smiled at him, the rest of the world faded from view.

"What are you two talking about?" Kelly asked as she wrapped her arms around his waist.

"Hawk was telling me what Edna May said when she heard we were marrying. It appears I was targeted."

Kelly laughed. "You should hear Mrs. Schattle over there. She's telling everyone who'll listen that she saved us."

"I'll give her that." He smiled down at her. "Who'd ever think I'd be glad for a nosy neighbor?"

Hawk laughed. "Watching you two scorch each other with your looks, I think I'll go find my wife. It gives me ideas."

Kelly blushed, but Ash laughed.

"Sounds like a good idea. Why don't we find a private place. I have an urge to kiss you."

She smiled. "I think I can find us a place. Follow me, Detective."

"I'll follow you anywhere, Kel. Anywhere."

* * * * *

Where Texas society reigns supreme—and appearances are everything.

Coming in June 2002
Stroke of Fortune by Christine Rimmer

Millionaire rancher and eligible bachelor Flynt Carson struck a hole in one when his Sunday golf ritual at the Lone Star Country Club unveiled an abandoned baby girl. Flynt felt he had no business raising a child, and desperately needed the help of former flame Josie Lavender. Though this woman was too innocent for his tarnished soul, the love-struck nanny was determined to help him raise the mysterious baby—and what happened next was anyone's guess!

Available at your favorite retail outlet.

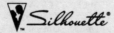

INTIMATE MOMENTS™

presents:

Romancing the Crown

With the help of their powerful allies,
the royal family of Montebello is
determined to find their missing heir.
But the search for the beloved prince
is not without danger—or passion!

Available in June 2002:
ROYAL SPY
by Valerie Parv (IM #1154)

Gage Weston's mission: to uncover a traitor in the royal family. But once he set his sights on pretty Princess Nadia, he discovered his own desire might betray *him*. Now he was determined to discover the truth about the woman who had grabbed hold of his heart....

This exciting series continues throughout the year with these fabulous titles:

Available only from Silhouette Intimate Moments
at your favorite retail outlet.

Silhouette®

Where love comes alive™

Visit Silhouette at www.eHarlequin.com

SIMRC6